When I woke up it was dark outside and felt hours later. I looked at the illuminated hands of my traveling clock: a quarter to ten. I sat up, listening. People went to bed early at Tradewinds, so I wasn't surprised not to hear anyone moving or people talking.

Getting out of bed I went to the door and listened. Then, slowly, I turned the doorknob and pulled. But the lock held. I was still trapped. Walking soundlessly in my sneakers, I went over to the window. Because of the bright moonlight, it was much brighter outside than in. I looked outside to see if Raoul was still there. He was. Still watching me.

I tried to think of ways to get out. If it weren't for Raoul, I could easily get down from my window. It was only the second floor.

Then I heard the faint click of the lock and soft footsteps going away from the door. In a second, I was there at the door, turning the knob. I gave a little pull, and the door opened. . . .

"An exotic setting, a plot with plenty of thrills, a little romance, and a group of memorable characters are skillfully combined to make *The Island* a good read."

Dallas Times Herald

THE ISLAND

Isabelle Holland

For Rosemary Courtney
from Isabelle Holland
with very best wishes

3.23.90

FAWCETT JUNIPER • NEW YORK

A Fawcett Juniper Book
Published by Ballantine Books
Copyright © 1984 by Isabelle Holland

Library of Congress Catalog Card Number: 84-11176

ISBN 0-449-70138-7

This edition reprinted by arrangement with Little, Brown & Company

The author is grateful to the *Marion County Record* for permission to use
the poem on page 135.

Manufactured in the United States of America

First Ballantine Books Edition: March 1986

THE ISLAND

Isabelle Holland

*For Rosemary Courtney
from Isabelle Holland
with very best wishes*

8.23.90

FAWCETT JUNIPER • NEW YORK

A Fawcett Juniper Book
Published by Ballantine Books
Copyright © 1984 by Isabelle Holland

Library of Congress Catalog Card Number: 84-11176

ISBN 0-449-70138-7

This edition reprinted by arrangement with Little, Brown & Company

The author is grateful to the *Marion County Record* for permission to use
the poem on page 135.

Manufactured in the United States of America

First Ballantine Books Edition: March 1986

1

The plane from New York took three hours, then I flew in a much smaller plane to the main island of this particular little archipelago, and took yet a third—the smallest of all—to the island where I was going to stay with my uncle and aunt.

As I sat in the tiny cabin of the plane which, in a push, might have held four, but where I was the only passenger, I looked down on the choppy blue-green water of the Caribbean Sea. Small islands, like little tufts of grass and reed rising out of the billowing sea, passed underneath. Some were dotted with cabins. Others were thick with tropical vegetation.

"Is it very hot?" I asked the pilot, a dark, silent young man with deeply tanned forearms and a bandit's mustache.

"Where? On Maenad? If there weren't a breeze, or, more accurately, a wind, it would be very hot indeed. But there's always a wind, so don't worry. Who are you visiting?"

"My uncle," I said. And then, "He's not actually an uncle. She—my aunt—is some kind of cousin of my mother's. They went to college together."

"Ever been here before?"

"No." We had to shout above the noise of the engines.

1

The propellers of the twin motors looked like discs, huge haloes guiding the plane.

"Do you live here?" I asked.

"No, I live on the chief island, Sibyl, one hundred miles north. It's bigger and more civilized, and they have a better airstrip." He was sitting in the pilot's seat with his back to me, of course. He glanced at me in a rearview mirror he had over the huge plate glass making up the windscreen. "How long are you staying?"

"I'm not sure. Maybe a week or two."

"You don't sound wildly happy about it."

"It's not that. It *does* sound wonderful." I added more formally, "I'm looking forward to it."

It was hard to explain my mixed-up feeling. It had all happened so fast: my bout with flu, the doctor saying I should get away for a while, and the letter from Aunt Louisa that seemed to arrive at exactly the right time. In it she begged Mother to let me come to their vacation home in Maenad for a week or two, to make up (as she wrote) for all the years she had failed in her duties as "a proper aunt."

The whole thing sounded heaven-sent: a tropical island, a great house that was practically a resort in itself with a pool, horses and a lot of young people.

And then, finally, if I went, Mother could go with Daddy to South America where he was going to do research for a book on indigenous guerrilla movements and give a guest lecture at the University in São Paulo. Mother could get the time from her job as a hospital laboratory assistant, and Juliet, my younger sister, was all set to go to her camp.

"You'll love it," Mother said. "Honestly, Hilda, at your age I would have pawned my soul to go." She looked at me for a moment. "Darling, if you don't want to go, you certainly don't have to."

"Coward!" Juliet said.

"I am not. Go stuff your head!" Even then I had a curious feeling of unease. Probably, I decided, I was just suffering from the post-flu blues, having had flu a month before. Because Maenad certainly sounded like anyone's description of holiday perfection. "I can't wait," I said firmly, resolving that was the way I felt.

But my last night at home, perhaps from a combination of nerves and excitement, I had, for the first time in years, my recurrent nightmare.

In my dream I was running down a long hall, clutching something, and pursuing a tall shadowy figure. I knew that if I didn't catch that figure I would die. I always woke up just as the figure disappeared—before I could catch up with it—and I would find my pillow soaked with tears or my nightgown wet with perspiration. My father always said it was something I ate. Mother said it was something or other in a developmental stage. Juliet wanted to know what the shadowy figure looked like.

"I don't know," I said. "He never turns around."

"Interesting," Juliet said in her most portentous voice. Juliet is eleven and very bright. She's already decided she's going to be a psychiatrist, but can't make up her mind between Freud and Jung. . . .

"There it is," the pilot said.

I looked out the window. Far below was the island, shaped like a rough cross, with vegetation so thick that the spaces where there were houses or other buildings looked as though they had been shaved.

Unlike other islands we'd flown over, Maenad seemed set off by itself, isolated.

"It looks remote," I said. "Most of the islands come in groups."

"Well, Maenad is governed by Sibyl, which is a hundred miles away. But you're right. It *is* stuck off by itself."

I wasn't sure what made me ask. "Do boats go there?"

"No. Not regularly."

"You mean it's the plane or nothing?"

He smiled. "That's right. It's the plane or nothing. Once you're on Maenad you're there until you can get a plane to take you off."

I stared down at the rapidly approaching island, trying not to feel a rising claustrophobia.

"It was British, wasn't it?" I said.

"Yes. It was originally discovered by one of the British pirates in the sixteenth century. He built a huge house where he could stash his stolen property and his various wives and children."

"Didn't they fight—the wives, I mean."

"According to legend, like cats and dogs. And some of them killed others. Eventually, not long after he built the place, the wives all died or ran away. Nobody knows what happened to the pirate. One day he rowed out from the ship in his dinghy and landed on the island. He was never seen again."

"Maybe one of his wives killed him."

"That's what the legend says: that his wives ganged up on him. But neither he nor his body was ever found."

"That's pretty strange. It's not a large island."

"True. And there've been lots of efforts to locate him. But nobody ever has. If he was as cruel as legend says, maybe it's best. Why go to the trouble and expense of digging him up?"

I shivered a little.

"Cold? There's a sweater over there you can put on."

"It's all right," I said quickly. "I'll be fine." I became aware of his eyes in the mirror, looking at me.

"How old are you?" he asked suddenly.

"Seventeen," I lied, adding on a few months for dignity.

"How old are you?" Something told me that without the mustache he'd be much younger—nearer my age.

"Well . . ." He glanced at me in the rearview mirror. "Guess!"

"Eighteen. Or nineteen."

He grinned. "On the nose."

"Which nose—eighteen or nineteen?"

"Somewhere between the two."

"Aren't you tremendously young to be piloting a plane?"

"On our island you can try for your license at seventeen. This isn't TWA." He gave another grin. "Anyway, my uncle owns this mini-airline. Want to have a drink after we land? Believe it or not, there's a really cool bar not far from the airport. Lots of the islanders go there." He paused. "But I guess someone's meeting you."

"I think Uncle Brace is."

"What's Uncle Brace's full name?"

"Brace Kingsmark."

"The man who owns all those rubber companies and corporations?"

"Well, he's managing director or something of some multinational outfit."

"Same thing."

There was a silence. I watched the island grow bigger as we slowly circled and started down. The closer we got the more the island looked like a blob and less like a cross. I could see the airstrip now, a tiny ribbon in a narrow area of grass. Lining the airstrip were low buildings.

"What are those buildings?" I asked.

"Hangars, warehouses—most of them your uncle's I should think. He's the only representative of big business on the island."

As we flew low on the approach, I saw a figure waiting beside a car parked near the airstrip.

"Is that your uncle?" the pilot said.

"I don't know. I've never met him."

We glided lower. The trees got larger and larger. A few feet above the ground I could pick out the palm and banana trees. As we slid down onto the runway, the pilot pushed his window open a little. And for the first time I could smell the island. The smell made real our presence in the subtropics. It was an unforgettable combination of lush, swampy earth, heavy-scented flowers and rotting vegetation. I took a great gulp of the warm sweet air. I knew in that moment that as long as I lived I would never forget that particular perfume.

The propellers stopped. The pilot waited until the blades slowed. Then he opened the door, pushed out the little steps and sprang out himself.

Standing on the airstrip was a tall young man with fair hair, and one of the most magnificent German shepherds I'd ever seen.

Because of my mother's allergy, none of us had ever had pets. But I loved animals and was determined, as soon as I had a place of my own, to have as many as I could. Picking up my sweater, I stepped out onto the concrete. The dog gave a low growl.

"Quiet, Wolf," the young man said, and he pulled on the chain that was around the dog's throat.

Without thinking, I walked straight to the dog. I had no fear, and I knew, somehow, that he wouldn't hurt me.

"Hello, Wolf," I said, and I held out my hand, which he sniffed. Then I patted his head.

Wolf got off his haunches, licked my hand again, wagged his tail and tried to jump up.

"Down, Wolf!" the boy said and jerked him again.

"Don't do that!" I cried. "He wasn't doing any harm."

"He must be trained."

"Trained for what?"

"As a guard dog, of course." Then he smiled. "For people who come from New York and have to have guard dogs to live in the city."

"We don't have any," I said. "And we walk out all the time."

The boy grinned. "Uncle Brace said you had a reputation for argumentativeness."

"Since I've never seen him I wonder how he knew."

He shrugged. "Probably your mother's letter via Aunt Louisa."

"Are they your uncle and aunt, too?"

"Yes. I'm Paul Kingsmark. And you're Hilda Tashoff."

"That's right. Then you're my cousin, sort of—at least by marriage. Did you come to meet me?"

"Yes. The Jeep's over there. Uncle Brace and Aunt Louisa are holding tea for us, so we'd better go. Where's your luggage?"

"Here," the pilot said, putting two bags down beside me. "Have a good ride home." He held out his hand.

Something, I didn't know what, made me ask suddenly, "What's your name?"

"Steve. Steve Barrington."

"Come along, Hilda. I told you. They're holding tea for us." Paul was frowning. Wolf made a slight move to come over, but Paul yanked him back. "Sit!" Paul said.

I was still holding Steve's hand. "Thanks for the ride," I said.

"A pleasure."

Paul put my bags in the back. Wolf jumped in beside them and I got in the front seat.

"Why don't you like Steve?" I asked.

"What makes you think I don't?"

"You weren't very friendly."

For a moment he didn't say anything. Then, "This is not

7

the States, you know. Things are a little more formal here.''
For the first time I noticed a faint accent. It was very slight,
and had as much to do with the way he spoke, as with the
actual pronunciation. "Where do you live?" I asked.
"Here?"

"Good heavens, no. You couldn't live here. There are no
schools for one thing.''

"None?"

"Well, not for us. The natives have one—mostly religious. But even they go to one of the larger islands if they
want to go beyond the eighth grade.''

"Well, where do you go to school?"

He mentioned a famous American prep school. "Before
that I went to boarding school in England." He turned and
grinned at me. "I've also lived in Guatemala, Argentina,
Germany and Italy.''

I burst out laughing. "You sound like the League of Na-
tions. If your father a diplomat?"

"No, he was some kind of international banker. I live
with my great-uncle.''

"Your father's dead?"

"Yes."

"And your mother?"

His smile faded. "We don't see each other. She lives
wherever the fast track is running. At the moment she's in
Switzerland.''

I thought instantly of my parents—not fast track people at
all. My father is an editor in a publishing house in New York
and Mother works in a hospital lab. I couldn't imagine them
without each other.

"That must seem strange," I said. "To have your mother
off somewhere—not at home.''

"It depends what you're used to. To me it's ordinary.''

He glanced sideways at me. "I take it you're a very together type family."

Something about the way he said it irritated me. "Very," I said. "The original nuclear household."

"Sounds confining."

I was about to make some snappy comeback when I remembered one of Mother's final parting statements: "Hilda, try, just try, not always to have the last word. I promise you, the world does not come to an end. And not having the last word does not mean total defeat. Besides," she said, beginning to look through her travelers checks, "it's much more mysterious to keep your own counsel. Makes people want to know what you think, instead of being always told."

So I folded my lips and decided to notice the scenery, which was passing by on either side. There wasn't a lot to notice, since trees of every kind lined the road, with palms towering above the others. Underneath were shorter trees and bushes so thick they looked like a green wall.

Finally I broke the silence.

"Is that all there is on the island? Just trees and undergrowth?"

"Almost all. There's sugarcane on the longer northern end—" He glanced at me and smiled, "on the tail of the cross. And some of the people have gardens where they grow vegetables and sell them locally, likewise a few chickens. But everything else has to be flown in."

At that moment I felt something soft on my shoulder and I looked around. Wolf had slid his muzzle next to my ear. Reaching back, I patted him. "He's a dear," I said.

"Wolf—sit!" Paul barked out.

The muzzle withdrew. I turned and saw Wolf poised on the seat as rigid and controlled as a grenadier. "Just because he's a guard dog doesn't mean he can't be affectionate."

9

"Uncle Brace is not training dogs to be affectionate. He's training them to be guard dogs. And this one is not going to graduate with high marks. We don't know why. His breeding is fine. But he keeps breaking discipline."

I looked back at Wolf's intelligent face. "Good for you!" I said.

Paul grinned. "You're not going to help him if you give him mixed messages."

"I just don't want him to think that everybody's a drill sergeant."

Wolf leaned forward and gave me a big lick. "See what I mean?" Paul said. "If Uncle Brace were in the Jeep, Wolf would get a wallop for that."

"Why is he such a bug about discipline? What does it matter? Do you have that much crime here?"

"No." Paul glanced at me. "I thought you knew. Guard dogs are trained here at Tradewinds. From a money point of view that's the island's biggest product—next to sugar, which is joined to the produce of all the other islands. We supply guard dogs to police, plants, factories, warehouses and private individuals."

"But I thought Uncle Brace was just here on holiday. Doesn't he live somewhere else—in Rome? And isn't he, like I said, the head of some huge company? He doesn't just train guard dogs, does he?"

Paul laughed. "Of course not. The guard dogs are only one among many of Uncle Brace's sidelines. He and Aunt Louisa do live in Rome, but he comes here quite often. He keeps an eye on the training and trainers."

"Oh." I tried to remember what Mother had said was in Aunt Louisa's letters. I hadn't read the letters myself, but when Mother talked about it, Maenad had sounded much more like one of the islands where tourism was the big industry, the place everybody went to on vacation.

"I thought Maenad was sort of an island vacation place, like one of the Virgin Islands or Antigua or the Bahamas."

The road started to climb a little. After a while the vegetation grew thinner until only the stately palms were left, their lacy heads blowing in the breeze. The incline became steeper. The road veered to the left, and I saw the line of palms rimming the edge of a high cliff. Beyond and far below that was the sea. It was both startling and magnificent. "Could you stop a minute so I can see?"

Paul brought the Jeep to a halt. I got out and walked to the edge. The slope below was covered with trees and bushes going straight down to the thin strip of sand and the green water. To my left, the land curved out, forming one of the arms of the cross, and the cliff opposite was much lower—in fact only a few feet above a much wider band of beach.

"You can see the whole island better from the house," Paul said from beside me.

A cold nose pressed against one of my hands. Without turning or stooping I stroked the side of Wolf's muzzle and the area between his ears. There was something about Wolf that made me believe he was miscast as a budding guard dog. On the other hand I didn't want to get him in trouble.

"Look the other way, behind you."

I turned and stared. The house, its windows glinting in the afternoon sun, was spread-eagled just below the peak of the island. But only the upper half could be seen. The house was surrounded by the same thick vegetation that lined the roads.

"It looks absolutely cut off among all those trees. Like something in the jungle," I said, and despite the warmth of the moving air, felt a chill.

"Oh, it's not as bad as that. The ground around the house is cleared more than you can see from here. There's a swimming pool in front, a tennis court, stables and a fair amount of garden. Come along now. We have to get back."

As we drove off I said finally, "Why would there be a tennis court if there are no other people—non-native people—on the island?"

"It can be a bit of a problem sometimes." There were moments when Paul sounded more than usually foreign, and this was one of them. "But often there's a large house party. You'll see. They come and go."

Something—I didn't know what—made me say sharply, "I'm not going to be here long enough to see, as you put it."

"Aren't you? My impression was that you'd be staying quite a long time."

"Where did you get that?"

"I don't know. Something Aunt Louisa said, probably."

"Well, she's wrong. I'm just staying . . . staying a week or two. Then I have to go home."

"Suit yourself. But I think you're crazy."

"Why? What's so great about being here? What do you do all day?"

"Everything. Help with the dogs, swim in the pool, play tennis, ride. Uncle Brace has some terrific horses, some of them part thoroughbred, and below the tennis court and swimming pool an area has been cleared and hurdles put up to practice show jumping."

"You have a horse show here?"

He laughed. "No, on Sibyl. We fly the horses there. A lot of the Brits keep their mounts on Sibyl. There's trail riding there and a pony club. Sibyl's been represented in Madison Square Garden," he said proudly.

"Sibyl sounds like a lot more fun." I thought about Steve Barrington, who lived there.

"Yes. But on Sibyl—well, there are lots of other people like us."

I looked at him for a moment. "You mean here you're the big cheese."

"Yes." He didn't hesitate about agreeing.

"At least you're honest."

"Hang on," he said, and swerved the steering wheel.

We swung again and started up a narrow road that was climbing steeply through trees that met overhead. It was much darker and there was no breeze. I could feel the sweat break out on my neck and back.

"And here we are," Paul said. With that we burst out of the trees and he pulled the car up.

In front of us was the house, a great white stone affair spread out on either side of a portico. In front of each side ran a porch supported by columns.

"How old is it?" I finally asked. Not that I really cared very much, but I had to say something to overcome the antipathy to the house that was growing in me by leaps and bounds. It was not ugly, yet—quite suddenly—I found myself hating and fearing it. Since I had never seen the house or the island, or even heard of them, I was even more frightened by the way I felt. With my entire being I wanted to go home, to my parents, to safety. Safety . . . ? I became aware that Paul had been talking, and that I had not heard a word. Perhaps, I thought, he hadn't noticed.

"Do you like it here?" I asked.

"Yes. I love being here. I'd stay all year round if they'd let me." He glanced at me. "You look funny. What's the matter?"

And the feeling, the fear, went away as suddenly as it had come. It was hard even to remember that I had felt that way. Now I was looking at a large but ordinary house that was fresh with new paint on both its brick front and its green shutters. Yet it was plainly not new. "How old is the house?" I asked, and then realized I'd asked it before.

"Weren't you listening? I just told you. This part, the part you see, is about a hundred years old, but it's resting on a much older part that was built at the end of the eighteenth century. And that one, they say, was built on an even older one put up by the pirate king. All his wives are supposed to be buried underneath. Come along, we'd better go."

The Jeep climbed the little road that followed the bordering line of trees until it got to the circular driveway, then turned and stopped in front of the shallow steps with a spray of gravel.

"Mademoiselle est arrivée," Paul said and got out of the car. "Come along, I'll take you in."

"What about my bags?"

"Oh, the servants will get those."

A gray-haired man in a white coat and black trousers came down the steps. "The bags are in the back, André," Paul said. "Are the others in the drawing room?"

"Yes, Mr. Paul."

We stepped onto the porch with its tile floor and then to the fanlight door. But at that moment it opened and a shortish man with black and gray hair came out. "Here you are," he said. "Welcome to Tradewinds, my dear Hilda. We've been looking forward to this for so long."

He took my hand and smiled. "Your Aunt Louisa is really eager to see you. Isn't she, Paul?"

"Absolutely," Paul said.

"But . . ." I wanted to say, How could she be? I'd never even heard of her, let alone seen her, before.

"But?" Uncle Brace said. He turned back and smiled at me. Then he put his hand under my elbow and guided me through the front door, across the hall and into the drawing room. Without being rude and abrupt, there was no way of explaining how curious this all was. I shook my head. "Nothing."

"Louisa will be here in a moment, and our houseguest. Ah," he said. "Here they are. Louisa, my dear. The long-awaited niece, the one you have been so looking forward to seeing, is here." Like Paul, Brace had a foreign intonation, or perhaps it was phraseology.

I stared at the woman coming slowly from the hall into the room. In appearance she was reassuring, because although she and Mother were not much alike, it was easy to see the resemblance. Mother had been a Godwin, and Godwins nearly always carried the identifiable family look: large nose, square jaw and slightly hooded dark eyes. Louisa Kingsmark had certainly been a Godwin. The nose was not quite as large as Mother's and the eyes were paler and more vague. But I found myself rushing up to her.

"Hello, Aunt Louisa," I said, astonished at how glad I was to see her. "It's wonderful to see you."

"Dear child," she said. Her face came forward and her lips brushed my cheek. "So happy you could come. Brace," Aunt Louisa said, going past me. "I haven't had tea."

"No, my dear, don't you remember? We were awaiting Hilda here. But now that she is with us, we can go ahead. Paul, why don't you ring the bell?"

It was while Paul was pulling the heavy and rather moth-eaten rope hanging beside the empty fireplace that someone else came in the room.

He was straight as a pine, but old. How old I couldn't be sure. And his eyes were bluer than any I had ever seen. He was, in fact, extremely handsome. Slowly and deliberately he walked towards me and I watched him, feeling a growing tension.

"Good afternoon," he said. His accent was quite strong. "My name is John Gomez."

I was aware of a feeling of surprise as I put my hand in

his. His hand was large and his fingers both long and strong. "And I'm Hilda Tashoff."

"Hilda," he said.

There was a silence. We stood there, my hand still in his. Then the silence was broken by the silvery tinkling of a little handbell.

"Tea," Aunt Louisa said. "Come along, Hilda."

2

I had only once before had tea that had been made with anything but a tea bag dangled in a cup of hot water. As Mother said, "Tea bags aren't elegant, but they're useful." And Father, who liked to read while he drank his tea, said "Elegant is a lot of trouble. In fact, it's a way of life."

The one exception was the afternoon Mother, Juliet and I had tea with Mother's formidable Great-aunt Sarah in her house on Beacon Hill in Boston. I was twelve and Juliet was seven, and I have forgotten why we were there. But the curving silver teapot, with the taller pot for hot water and the cream jug and sugar bowl, all in the same ornate pattern of grapes and leaves, remained in my mind. As did one sentence or statement: "Of course," Aunt Sarah said to me, pouring hot water on top of the dark tea, "your father is Jewish." What led up to it, what was said afterwards, is gone. There was neither severity nor disapproval in Aunt Sarah's statement. But I remember feeling uncomfortable, as though I had said or done something wrong. I also remember staring at the tea and wishing it were a soda.

Now, here, in another drawing room, was another beautifully chased teapot. The design here was smaller, more delicate, and the hot water pot was plain.

"How do you take your tea, Hilda?" Aunt Louisa asked.

I had no idea. Tea was tea. "Nothing special, Aunt Louisa," I said.

"Lemon or milk?"

"Er—milk." I was one of the few people who didn't like lemon.

"Sugar?"

"Yes, please." I eyed the little cubes. "Two lumps."

"You take your tea the way the English do," Uncle Brace said, bringing the cup across to me.

"I don't know. I've never been to England."

"That should be remedied," Mr. Gomez said. "A civilized nation."

"Ha—John," Aunt Louisa said. Her voice faltered. Her dark eyes sought her husband's. He was frowning.

"I think I will have mine like Hilda's," Mr. Gomez said, and taking his teacup from Aunt Louisa, he came and sat beside me.

"How was your journey?" Mr. Gomez said.

"Fine," I said. "Especially the last part—in the small plane."

"Yes, flying a small aircraft is very different from being in a 747."

Something about the way he said that made me ask, "Do you fly your own plane?"

"Yes, sometimes, though not as often as I used to."

"I sat right behind the pilot, Steve Barrington. I could see everything he did. It was exciting. He was very smooth, very, very . . ." I was looking for the right word.

"Competent?" Mr. Gomez said, smiling.

"Yes."

"Yes, he is good."

"Do you know him?"

"He has flown me here on visits. He's a good pilot. He's a native, of course."

"Is that bad?"

"No, no." The blue eyes were on me. "I didn't mean that at all. It's just—the natives live such separate lives."

"Why?"

He didn't answer right away, but stirred his tea. Then he looked up at me. "I keep forgetting. You live in New York. The world's great melting pot. But tell me, where do you go to school?"

"At Brendan School."

"A private school?"

"Yes."

"Religious?"

I laughed. "No. Not at all. My father's Jewish. Mother's Episcopalian. Any religious school for me is out."

Aunt Louisa was getting up. "Dinner will be at eight," she said. "You can rest in your room after you've changed."

"Changed?" I said.

"Yes." She looked a little bewildered for a moment. "You did bring another dress?"

"Yes, I'll . . . er . . . put another one on. I have to un-pack, too."

"Oh, Williams will have done that. But you'll want a bath." She smiled vaguely. Her eyes were more hazel than brown, but they were very like Mother's. I said quickly, "Can I come and talk to you for a few minutes, Aunt Louisa?" If we talked, I thought, maybe the growing sense of strangeness would go away.

"Of course—" she started, and then faltered and looked towards her husband.

He came over and took my hand. "My dear, you must help us be part of a conspiracy. Your Aunt Louisa hasn't been at all well, and we want her to get as much rest as possible. I'm sure you understand.''

"Yes, of course," I said. "But all I want—"

"No tensions, no problems." His voice, smooth as oil, went right over me. "That's what our doctor insisted on. And we must, of course, abide by what he says." He pressed my hand. "You and I will have that talk, I promise you. You understand?" It was posed as a question and yet, I felt, it was a demand.

"Yes," I said. But I didn't. Rebuffed and confused, I looked at Aunt Louisa, who was walking slowly to the door.

He patted my hand. I took it away. "I'll go upstairs," I said. And then, to lighten the queerly stiff atmosphere, "Do I turn right or left?"

He touched a bell beside the empty fireplace. "Just a minute. Williams will show you to your room."

In a moment a woman with iron gray hair and a severe expression came in.

"Williams, would you show Miss Hilda to her room, and help her with any unpacking she has to do."

"Her unpacking has been done, sir. I will be glad to show her the way to her room."

As I followed the woman upstairs I examined her stiff back. She had on a black dress with a high neck and long sleeves. Her stockings were dark and her shoes were flat.

I followed the woman into the left wing. She stopped before a door, opened it, and then stood aside for me to go in. Feeling like a fool, I went in ahead of her.

The room had the same spacious quality as the drawing room downstairs. Suddenly I knew why the rooms seemed different: the ceilings were extremely high, and would have looked even higher if there hadn't been giant fans hung in the ceiling.

"Your things have been put in the closet and the bureau,

Miss Hilda. Your suitcases are downstairs in the boot room. If there's anything I can do, the bell is over there, beside the bed. Would you like me to run your bath?''

"No thanks," I said quickly. The sooner I could be alone the better. Everything in the house seemed strange, and this woman most unsettling of all.

"Very well, miss." And she withdrew.

I let out my breath and stared around the room. The bed was wide, with brass head and foot, and stood out from the wall a foot or so. There were grass or straw mats on the floor. There were a desk, a bureau with four drawers, a small table, a chair and another small table beside it. An open door on the other side of the bed showed a little of the white tile that I assumed to be a bathroom.

Slowly I walked over to the window and stared into the thick green of the trees that rose not far away. The room obviously faced the back, because the land sloped up from the window and the vegetation was close around.

I looked at my watch. Five-fifteen. Dinner at eight. A sense of loneliness washed over me. I wished suddenly I wasn't in this weird place among strange, rather foreign people. "Hilda—don't make up your mind so fast. . . ." I could hear Mother saying the words. She'd said them often enough before. "Give it a little time. . . ." The memory gave me a pang of homesickness.

In the meantime, I thought, sighing, and turning away from the window, there were almost three hours to kill. And it was true, I was tired at the end of three separate airplane rides. Should I take my bath now, or my nap first? I was trying to make up my mind between these earthshaking options when I heard what sounded like a soft whimper. I held my breath. Yes, there it was again. And there was a soft scratch on the door.

21

Then I heard down the hall, in a voice I didn't recognize, "Wolf! Wolf! Come here at once!"

Moving rapidly across the floor I opened my door a crack. A black and tan muzzle pushed through. I opened the crack a little wider and Wolf came in only just in time. The voice was approaching down another corridor at a right angle to the one where I was standing. Very quietly I closed the door, and, with my hand on Wolf's head, heard the voice, still calling, pass my door and quickly disappear down another hall.

"Saved!" I whispered, and knelt down in front of Wolf. He licked my face and I hugged him. I'd always loved animals; but never in my life had I been so glad to see one. In this strange place he was a friend. And I felt I needed one.

Wolf sat on the bath mat beside the tub while I took my bath and then napped next to me on the bed afterwards. Every now and then he'd wake up and start licking my face.

When I left the room, he stood in the hallway and watched me as I made my way down the hall towards the staircase. It was quite obvious that he knew he wasn't allowed where I was going.

"G'bye," I whispered and waved. As I went downstairs I hoped he wouldn't get into any trouble.

There was a mirror at the bottom of the stairs and I checked to make sure everything was in place—something I'd forgotten to do in my bedroom, partly because I overslept, and partly because I was too busy paying attention to Wolf. My blonde hair had been cut just before I had left New York, so it now waved only to my shoulders. The fact that it was curly instead of straight had always been a sore point; all the hair I had admired on other girls had been fine and straight and looked as though it had been ironed. Mine was heavier, thicker and permanently sun streaked.

My royal blue sleeveless tunic dress made my eyes look bluer. A light, dense blue, they were my most prominent feature. For the rest of me, I was tall and rather narrow— totally unlike any other member of the family, although Mother assured me I looked like my great-grandmother on her side of the family. Since there were no photographs, I had to take her word for it. Mother, Father and Juliet were all dark-haired and dark-eyed, and although Father was of medium height and wiry, Mother and Juliet were medium to short, and were distinctly curvier.

"You look charming," a voice said behind me, and then I saw Mr. Gomez' reflection.

"Thank you."

He came over and stood beside me, an erect, handsome man in dinner jacket, his gray hair still thick.

For a moment we stood there, smiling at one another. And then, from nowhere, came the growing feeling of unease I had felt before pushing at the doors of my conscious mind.

"Shall we go into the drawing room?" he asked.

"Yes, all right."

As though it were a natural thing, he took my hand and led me in. "And here is our guest of honor," he said, as we came into the room.

The rest stood frozen for a moment, reminding me of school tableaux where the curtain would go up for a minute or two, and then come down again.

Then Uncle Brace moved forward. "And did you have a good nap?" he inquired.

"Yes thanks. Fine. I—" I stopped on the brink of telling him about Wolf. Perhaps my uncle wouldn't have approved of his playing hookey from his training like that. Paul across the room was also in a black tie, which made him look suddenly grown up. He was, I finally decided, about nineteen.

"Hi," he said, coming over. "What would you like to drink?"

"A sherry perhaps?" Mr. Gomez said.

"Thanks. I'd rather have a soda."

"Come on, Hilda, don't be a square. You're seventeen. Time to grow up. Here's some sherry for you." And Paul handed me a small, delicately cut sherry glass. Gingerly I took a sip. I had occasionally had a sip from my parents' wine and never really liked it. I liked sherry even less. But I certainly didn't want to seem like the Ugly American, so I kept it in my hand while I decided whether it would be better to try and have a talk with my Aunt Louisa now or later.

For a moment she seemed to be by herself, and was staring down at her own wineglass which she held with both hands. Unlike the rest of us, she was seated in an armchair. There really was no reason why I shouldn't walk straight over to my aunt, and sit down in the chair next to her armchair. Yet something told me that such a direct approach might not achieve what I wanted. So I started sidling slowly around the men who seemed to be all talking at once about some situation or other in Latin America, and finally found myself beside my aunt's chair.

"Aunt Louisa," I said rather softly.

She looked up. "Hello, my dear. Is everything all right? Room in order?" Her voice dragged a little. She must be terribly tired, I thought.

"Yes. It's fine." I tried to think then how to continue. I'd have liked to have led up slowly to what I wanted to ask, which was why was I here? But I was fairly sure that we'd be interrupted and I didn't want to blurt my questions out in front of everybody. I was turning over various starts in my mind when she gave me an opening.

"I do hope you're having a good time, my dear," she said in her whispery voice.

"It's different from what I—we, Mother and I—thought,"
I said.

She surprised me then. "Yes. I knew how you'd find it. I
told Brace . . ." Her slightly faded hazel eyes looked up
quickly in her husband's direction.

"I thought it'd be sort of like . . . well, like staying at the
beach," I finally burst out in a whisper. "You know, with
lots of kids . . ." To my own ears I was sounding rude and
critical, and I could imagine what Mother would say, but I
was certain she envisioned the island as I had.

"I told your mother—"

"Now what are you two whispering about?" Uncle Brace
said. "We can't let the ladies go off to themselves like that.
Hilda, come here and tell us what you think about some of
the plans Paul has."

Reluctantly I got up, irritated that I was being prevented
from talking to Aunt Louisa, and tempted to say so. Yet
there was something—some inhibition preventing me from
doing what I so often did in my life—blurting out what was
on my mind.

Uncle Brace put his hand on my arm. "I thought we'd get
some people over from Sibyl for a day or two and have
round-robin tennis interspersed with swimming. What do
you think?"

I was startled by how much the thought of other people
brought a sense of relief.

"That'd be terrific," I said. "Would they stay here?"

"They don't have to stay. They can fly here early in the
morning, bringing bathing suits and tennis things, and fly
back at night. Barrington can chauffeur them. But if they
wanted to stay, there's plenty of room for them."

"I think it's a marvelous idea," I said with enthusiasm.
'Are you going to phone them?"

He grinned and the others laughed. "You don't realize

quite how primitive we are in some ways. No, Paul will go down to the radio station in the village and do it via two-way radio.''

''You mean you don't have a telephone?''

''Quelle horreur!'' Uncle Brace exclaimed, and held up his hand in mock dismay. ''What a child of the twentieth century you are! Yes, we have a phone. Unfortunately, our last storm damaged the wires, so we are temporarily without. But a man from the village is coming to mend it sometime next week. Paul here can do his invitations over the two-way radio.''

As we went in to dinner I thought grimly that Uncle Brace was right. I was a child of the twentieth century. And the idea of being in this bizarre house with these strange people without a phone struck me as the most frightening thing of all.

''Come,'' Mr. Gomez said, holding out a chair from the highly polished dining table. ''Give me the great pleasure of sitting beside me.''

It was the strangest meal I've ever had. For one thing, there were about five courses: soup, a little piece of fish, some chicken, a small piece of meat and a dessert. And there were five pieces of silver at each place setting. It was easy to figure out which was the soupspoon. After that as I stared with my hands hovering over the array of knives and forks, Mr. Gomez whispered, ''Start at the outside and work in.''

''Thanks,'' I whispered back, and smiled.

He smiled in response. It was a nice smile, lifting one side of his mouth. I decided that of all the people there, including Paul, he seemed the most human.

Uncle Brace and Mr. Gomez talked about South American politics, about training dogs, and about living in Rome.

"What do you do in Rome?" I asked Uncle Brace, when there was a pause in the conversation.

He lowered his wineglass. "I have my own import-export firm," he said. "For instance, I import coffee which John Gomez grows on his plantation."

"Where is your plantation?" I asked. Plantations, I thought, went out with the Civil War. But of course that was in the States.

"Brazil. You must come and visit it sometime. I can show you the coffee growing."

"That'd be fun," I said. Normally I'd be excited over visiting Brazil. I'd always loved the idea of travel, but my lack of enthusiasm at the thought made me realize how uneasy I was at being here, on Maenad Island, as though . . . as though, but my mind balked at whatever the next step was. I'd never had this experience before, but my mind seemed like a computer, that refused to obey when I pushed the button or the key marked "Imagine." Whatever it was had something to do with my parents and why I was here and was very disturbing.

"You are looking thoughtful," Mr. Gomez said. The cobalt blue eyes were on me. "Is everything all right?"

"I was just . . . I was just thinking about my parents."

There was a tiny pause. "They are well, I trust?"

"Yes. They're fine. At least I think they are. They're away. Which is why I'm here. Only . . ."

"Only what?"

I hesitated, because I really didn't know him very well, and what I was going to say seemed rude to Aunt Louisa and Uncle Brace. Despite all this I burst out, "It really isn't at all the way I'm sure Mummy and Daddy thought it was here. I mean, I thought, at least Mummy seemed to imply, that this would be sort of like staying with friends up on the Cape or in Nantucket. I mean, they're not poor or anything—the friends I mean—but it isn't so . . . so *formal*, sort of *grand*."

"I expect it's because your uncle and aunt have lived so long abroad. I know they want you to have a good time. And when . . . if . . . you come and visit me, you'll find our ranch much more the way you're used to. Much less formal."

I was astonished to hear myself say, "I couldn't come without my family." —I who had always been so independent!

There was a pause. "You are very devoted to your family?"

As I stared at him, at the strangeness of his question, he said quickly, "But of course. You have been with them for so long."

"Been with them—?" I couldn't help it, I laughed. "Sorry for laughing, but it's such a strange way of putting it. I've been with them, as you say, almost seventeen years."

"Ah, yes. Where were you born?"

"In New York."

"I see. In a hospital. All Americans are born in hospitals, aren't they?"

"Yes. At least, I suppose so. Unless they're born on the Hollywood Freeway because they didn't make the hospital on time. That's an American joke," I added hastily. "Yes, I was born in . . ." Queer, I thought. Mother hadn't ever actually told me the hospital, although I knew that Juliet arrived in New York Hospital. "Juliet—my sister—was born in New York Hospital, so I suppose I must have been, too."

"But your mother didn't tell you where?"

"No. I guess it just never came up."

He smiled again. "Ask her sometime."

"Come along, you two," Paul said. "You've been talking together much too long. What are all the secrets about?"

As he spoke he reached his hands towards the carafe of red wine that was in front of him. A carafe of white was in front of Mr. Gomez. As Paul grasped the carafe of red, Uncle Brace's hand suddenly shot out and took hold of Paul's wrist. "We must leave some for the kitchen," he said in a sort of jolly tone. But his eyes were narrow and rather hard.

"Are you trying to stop me?" Paul asked, his voice sulky.

"As I said, we must leave some for the servants."

"That's crazy!" Either on account of the wine or because Paul was excited, the trace of accent in his voice sounded much thicker. His hand was still out, with Uncle Brace's fingers around his wrist. As I watched, I saw the fingers tighten, and Paul's arm jerk. "All right," he muttered. "You don't have to get nasty." He pulled his arm back. Uncle Brace's fingers loosened and his hand dropped. Paul rubbed his wrist.

"How wise of you not to drink," Mr. Gomez said to me. "I expect your parents don't want you to."

"Well, they don't drink much themselves. Besides, I really don't like the taste."

"Miss Goody Two-Shoes," Paul sneered from across the table.

"Better than liking it too much," I snapped back.

"Paul—you will leave the table at once," Uncle Brace said.

Paul got up, wove a bit, made an elaborate bow towards Aunt Louisa. Then he said to me, "Goodnight, Goody Two-Shoes."

"At once!" Uncle Brace said.

I thought Paul was behaving like an idiot, but I also hated to see him publicly embarrassed by Uncle Brace. "You don't have to do that for me," I said. "I can stick up for myself."

"Paul is my responsibility," Uncle Brace said. "He must learn to behave properly."

I stared down at the dessert that arrived.

"You do not think Paul should learn to hold his wine like a gentleman?" Mr. Gomez asked.

"I think it's mean to put down somebody in front of other people." Although it was a large table and I was several feet away from Uncle Brace, I didn't care whether he heard me or not.

Obviously he did because he said, "Perhaps we are stricter in Europe than you are in America. American children are notoriously—relaxed—in their behavior."

Suddenly, and for the first time, Aunt Louisa spoke. Her voice was still thready, and her words were a little slurred, but she said quite clearly, "But there's nothing wrong with American money, is there?"

There was a short, electric silence. I wanted to giggle, and I also wanted to go over and kiss her. But I couldn't quite get up the courage to do either.

"My dear, you are feeling ill again. I told you you should let us send up a tray. Pedro—" Uncle Brace looked at the man who was hovering with a tray—"ask Williams to come at once."

The gray, granitelike woman who had shown me to my room appeared so quickly that I wondered if she was outside.

"Please help Mrs. Kingsmark upstairs," Uncle Brace said. Then, "Go, my dear," he said to Aunt Louisa.

Slowly she got to her feet, and leaned with one hand on the chair.

At that point a man I had not seen before appeared in the doorway. "Telephone, Mr. Kingsmark."

"I told you—" Uncle Brace snapped.

"I thought the telephone was broken," I said.

Uncle Brace glanced swiftly at me. "Obviously, it has been repaired."

"It is urgent," the man said.

"Very well, Emil. Williams, see to Mrs. Kingsmark. Ha—John, you'd better come with me." And Uncle Brace and Mr. Gomez left with the man.

"Hilda—" Aunt Louisa said. She still sounded fuzzy, but there was an urgency to her voice. "Hilda, there's something I must tell you—"

I saw Mrs. Williams' hand grip Aunt Louisa's arm. "Ah, Mrs. Kingsmark. You are not feeling well. Now you must lean on me as we go upstairs. Miss Hilda—perhaps you'd be good enough to get your aunt's sweater—it's in the drawing room. Bring it to us when we get to the stairs. Mrs. Kingsmark may need it later."

I ignored her and looked directly to Aunt Louisa. "What is it you were going to tell me?" I asked.

But it was as though she hadn't spoken. "What?" she asked. "Nothing—nothing at all. Williams, help me upstairs. I don't feel well."

For a moment I considered going up to her and trying to force her to talk to me. But I knew it would be no use. One thing was quite clear: Aunt Louisa was afraid of Williams, and all I could do would be to make things worse.

3

I lay in bed that night with the breeze flowing through the room, bringing the smell of the island warm and sweet. There were screens on the windows. Even so, I started off with the tall, filmy mosquito curtains pulled around the bed. But I found I hated them. They cut off my glimpse of the high moon and the trees swaying across it. So after a while, I sat up and pulled them back and trusted that the screens would be enough of a shield. Then I put my arms around my knees, and let the disturbing thoughts roll through my head:

Thought number one was that Uncle Brace had probably lied about the phone being out of order. It was possible, of course, that the wires had been fixed. If he remembered, he would probably tell me they had. But there was nothing about him that made me want to believe him.

The second thought was really more of a feeling—a sense of outrage and bewilderment at my parents for allowing me to come to such a place. If they truly didn't know what kind of place it was, why didn't they somehow find out? The only possible answer to that was that they didn't know, and had no reason to suspect that Aunt Louisa was misleading them. She had described the island in such glowing colors that they obviously assumed it would be like my staying with Kitty

Bernstein's family at the Vineyard as I had two years before. . . . That had to be the explanation, because the
alternative—that Mother and Father, knowing how weird
this place was, how awful the people, and how out of it Aunt
Louisa was, would send me here by myself—was totally un-
acceptable. They wouldn't do that. . . . *They wouldn't.* . . .

I put my head on my knees and let my mind float. . . .
What it floated to was something that had happened a month
before at home in our apartment in New York. Curious, I
thought, I hadn't consciously remembered it until now.

Daddy and I were joking about something at breakfast—I
couldn't recall now what it was about, but that was because
we joked a lot of the time. I love both parents, but I've
always been closest to Daddy. We have the same slightly
offbeat sense of humor, like the same things, such as the
Mets, summer concerts in Central Park, and jogging, and
are liable to get worked up about the same pro-people
causes.

Anyway, we were laughing away when Father picked up
one of the letters that had come in the mail and slit it open.
Afterwards, I tried to recall what country the stamp was
from. I knew it was foreign, and I thought it was from somewhere in South America. But I didn't really notice. Anyway, Daddy started to read the letter. His face went still and
then white.

"Hey—what's the matter?" I said.

He didn't answer. And suddenly, for no reason that I
could think of, I was frightened. "Seen a ghost or something?" I said, but my voice didn't sound amused. It
sounded scared. I'd never seen Father look like that. Suddenly he shoved the letter in his pocket and got up.

"So soon?" Mother said. "You'll give your office heart
failure if you turn up this early." She said it jokingly, but
then she saw Daddy's face and her own went still.

"Yeah, well, it'll keep them on their toes," Father said. He picked his manuscript case off the chair in the dining room and started towards the door.

"Daddy," I said suddenly. "What was in that letter?"

"Nothing for you to worry about," he said.

It was after that that he changed. He became aloof. I'd never seen him abstracted and rather silent that way before—

"Hey—it's me," I said once, when I'd addressed him twice without any reply. "Your once and future daughter, in case you'd forgotten."

He glanced at me, and for a moment, his dark eyes started to crinkle at the corners, the way they always did when he was about to say something funny or affectionate or both. But then they changed. "I haven't forgotten," he said in an odd voice, and left the room.

"What's the matter with Daddy?" I asked Mother.

"Oh, you know how he is when he has a book on his mind."

But Daddy had always told me about the books and authors he'd been working with, that is, since I was old enough to know what a book was. I tried a frontal assault. "What's the new book about?" I asked him that evening.

"What book?"

"The one you're so abstracted about."

"There's no book."

"I thought you were doing a book on guerrillas."

"No . . . yes . . . that has nothing to do with . . . with anything."

"Then why're you so—"

"Stop asking me questions. I'm tired of being badgered." And he stalked out of the room to his study.

"Don't have grudges," Father had said to me when I was quite small. "If you're mad about something, say so. We'll talk about it." And that's what we'd always done. Naturally, this had produced one or two major battles along the way. One memorable time was when I was offered the role of Portia in the school play.

"No," he had shouted. "I don't care if it is Shakespeare. It's anti-Semitic, and I'm not going to have my daughter up there addressing Shylock as 'Therefore, Jew, though justice be thy plea, consider this—' "

"But there are lots of Jews in the cast. Donna Rosenthal—"

"If their parents don't mind that's their business. But I do mind, and I'm surprised at you. Have you read the play? Have you read the background of how Jews were treated then?"

"But Shylock is the only interesting character in the play. The rest are either boring or stuffy."

"If you want to do it, go ahead. But don't talk to me about it. And don't expect me to turn up to see it." He grunted, "Your Episcopalian mother can do that."

"That should put me in my place," Mother said calmly.

Father stormed out of the room.

"I didn't know he had such a thing about being Jewish," I said to Mother.

"Barbara Rozinsky says we're not Jewish unless our mothers are," Juliet said, slowly putting marmalade on her English muffin.

"Yes, well," Mother said. "Your father had a bad experience with *The Merchant*. He was one of three Jewish boys in the school he went to, and when they did the play in class, he had to take a lot of clumsy and rather unkind humor about it. On the other hand, I went to a school that was mostly Jewish, and *The Merchant* was done with plenty of discussion about the historic background, and there was no major flak. It's up to you, Hilda."

I didn't take part in the school play that year. I still didn't understand why Daddy went off like a firecracker whenever it was mentioned, but to do the play knowing how he felt, and knowing that he wouldn't come to see it, wouldn't have been any fun, so I skipped it. The Tashoff method of dealing with problems—being open about them, and talking them out however noisily—had worked. I didn't resent not being in the play, and Father took me to Shakespeare in the Park that summer.

So about two weeks after the letter arrived and of Father's acting like a ghost around the place, I confronted him.

"Remember the great family method of dealing with problems? Lots of talk, maybe some yelling, but no casebuilding or hoarding? Well, you aren't acting the way you've always told us to act."

For a minute, I thought it was going to be okay. He stopped, put his hands on my shoulders and looked me in the eyes . . . and then his face changed again, the way I had seen it before. He turned around and walked away.

"Is it something I've done?" I asked Mother.

"No. It isn't. Just leave it alone, honey."

"Then it's something about me." I didn't know where that statement came from. All of a sudden it was there.

"Mother—!" I said.

"No, no, no, Hilda. Now leave it alone. You know adults can't share every last thing with their children. Let it go."

It was a few days after that that Aunt Louisa's letter arrived, and it seemed as though I was bundled off immediately afterwards, although there was an exchange of several letters between Mother and Aunt Louisa, and it was actually about a month.

A month, now as I looked back on it, of odd silences and tensions.

Once, as I was coming down the hall towards the living

room, I heard Father say, "I have to find out the truth—I don't need you for that. You can track down your cousin."

"I'd like to very much," Mother said in her clear voice. "I don't at all want—But I'm more concerned about you than anything. I feel—" And at that moment I entered the living room.

"What cousin?" I asked. "Cousin Louisa?"

There was a second's silence. "No," Mother said. "Cousin Marcia, living in Rio. Her husband's at the embassy there."

Juliet came bounding in then with something on her mind and the subject passed.

Until this moment I hadn't remembered it.

Now I wondered again. I knew Mother had a cousin in South America. But I didn't believe it was the cousin she was talking about. Neither of my parents had ever lied to me. If they didn't want to tell me something they said so. But they never lied.

Nevertheless, I was gripped with a conviction that the cousin Mother was referring to was Louisa. . . .

Then, as another memory assailed me, I raised my head and let go my knees, sliding my legs back down on the bed so that I was sitting with them straight.

"You'd think," Mother had said in that last week, when she was making the arrangements for my visit, "that they'd be reachable by telephone. But it seems the phone is broken."

But the phone wasn't broken, or had been mended. . . . Back to point one. If it hadn't been broken, then why would Uncle Brace lie about it?

It was at that point in my cogitations that I heard a faint scratch. I'd been leaning back on my hands, but I sat bolt upright and listened. Nothing. I'd just about decided that it was my imagination when the scratch came again, followed by a small whimper. Then I heard footsteps crunching in the gravel outside my window, and a man's voice, low but angry, "Wolf! Where are you? Come here at once!"

Sliding out of bed I went to the door and opened it a crack. A dark shape slithered in. I closed the door. The next thing I knew a pair of paws was on my shoulders and a warm tongue was licking my cheek.

"Wolfie!" I whispered. Then I hugged him, and got another kiss. "Now stay down," I whispered, and walked in bare feet over to the window.

"Wolf!" the man's voice said. I could hear his frustration at not being able to yell, given the late hour. And I could see his back. It was none of the men I'd met so far. But beyond that I could tell nothing. Beside me, Wolf sat, and as I put my hand on his side, I could feel a little tremble.

"Don't worry, Wolfie, you can spend the night here."

After that I went back to bed. Wolf stretched out beside me, and I went to sleep.

The problem, I realized the next morning, was whether to let Wolf stay in my room, where he would be safe, but where he would be discovered by the maid that was surely due to come in. Or to let him out, and expose him to the trainer's anger. There was also the little matter of his personal needs. He hadn't been out since the night before. I compromised, therefore, by leaving my door open a crack. When Wolf's face showed through, I leaned down and kissed him between his ears.

Aunt Louisa was not at breakfast. Nor was Paul. But Uncle Brace and Mr. Gomez were.

"We must show you the island today," Uncle Brace said. "Gomez and Paul and I."

I felt like asking about Paul, but after the embarrassing evening before I thought I'd better not.

"And then we must ask those people Louisa mentioned. Paul will do that as soon as he comes down."

"Is he all right?" I asked, before I could stop myself.

"Oh, fine. He's your average young man, occasionally drinks a little too much, but he has a good head on his shoulders."

It was at that moment that I heard a terrible yelp, and then another, followed by shouting in the loud version of the voice I'd heard the night before. There was another yelp and another and then one of the worst sounds in the world—something like a puppy screaming.

I leaped to my feet. "That's Wolf. I know it is." And I dashed out of the dining room, into the hall, out the front door and onto the driveway. The dreadful sounds were coming from the right, so I tore through some shrubbery, onto a lawn, saw some wire netting and low houses or kennels further off, behind a row of palms. Wolf was still yelping, but now there was the sound of barking also and growls. I ran through trees, and saw a man, whip in his hand, facing Wolf who was tied up to a post, with his paw caught in some kind of a vise.

"And you will learn—" the man said, raising his whip.

"Stop!" I yelled. "Stop that at once. How dare you beat him like that?"

He turned. I saw a dark, sunburned face, blue eyes and light brown hair. "Who the—Go back at once! This area is off limits. What are you doing on this property?"

"What are you doing beating that dog?"

"He is disobedient and must be trained. He got out last night—who knows where he spent the night. He is the worst of the last litter, but he *will* be disciplined! Now get away!"

I really didn't know what to do, but I didn't stop to think, anyway. I ran towards the man and reached up to his whip arm. "You won't touch Wolf again. I won't let you."

He gave me a mighty shove, and I staggered towards the post and against Wolf.

"Very well," the man said. "If you want a beating—some women do!" And he raised the whip again.

This time Wolf let out a ferocious growl and lunged at the man as far as his tether would let him. But the cruel whip caught him across the face, and the yelp of agony broke out of Wolf, who started pawing his face. Oh my God, I wondered, did that awful beast catch Wolf's eye?

"You rotten bully—see what you've done."

The man grinned. The whip went back again. I turned my back, holding Wolf on the other side of me.

"What on earth—? Put that whip down this minute!" It was Uncle Brace's voice.

I turned. Uncle Brace and Mr. Gomez were stalking up. "Surely," Mr. Gomez said, "you don't train your dogs like that. They must be disciplined, yes. But this is barbarism!" He turned towards Uncle Brace. "You led me to believe—"

"Yes, yes, all right. Schmidt here is inclined to overdo the whip. But he's right about the proper discipline. When these dogs leave here they'll attack anything that moves if they're hired to guard a house or factory."

"That is still no excuse to mistreat them. I've trained dogs myself. They must be trained to attack if told. But they must never be made into monsters through fear and pain. And that is just what is being done. I won't have it!"

"Look—maybe I was a little tough," Schmidt said. "He's always slipping out, and I'm supposed to deliver six fully trained dogs by the end of the month. If I deliver only five, I'll get paid a lot less. Not just the fifth less. That was in the agreement."

"I won't have Wolf made into a monster." I turned to my uncle. "I'm going to go back to New York today, and when she comes back, I'll tell my mother what it's really like here. And how Aunt Louisa is some kind of a zombie, or sick, or mental or something.''

His eyes narrowed. His face grew suddenly red. For a moment his mouth was a thin line. Then: ''Look, I told you Louisa is not well. Don't press me for more details. It wouldn't be right, and it wouldn't make your mother any happier to know the truth. I—we thought—that if you came here then perhaps she might recover a little.''

''I don't believe it.''

''I have a solution,'' Mr. Gomez said. ''Wolf shall be given to Hilda as her very own. No one else shall touch him, and when . . . when she goes back to New York, she will take him with her.''

There was a short silence. Then, ''What a wonderful idea!'' Uncle Brace said. ''Loose the dog, Schmidt.''

''I've told you, I'm supposed to deliver six dogs—''

Uncle Brace said something very rapidly in another language. After a moment I realized it was German. Schmidt shrugged and started towards the post.

''I'll untie him,'' I said. ''And I'll take his paw out of that trap.''

''It's only just a few teeth to keep him in line.''

''I'd like to put your foot in it for an hour or so! When my mother hears about this—she'll be *sick*.''

I finally untied Wolf and lifted his paw out of the twin rows of teeth. Parting them was simply a matter of turning a little wheel.

As I turned to lead Wolf back, I saw the whip lying on the ground. The temptation to pick it up and give Schmidt a taste of his own training was almost more than I could withstand. But I decided he might find a way to take it out on Wolf.

As I passed him I smelled liquor on his breath. ''You're drunk,'' I said, disgusted.

41

I turned to Mr. Gomez. "Thanks for Wolf. It's really great having him."

Mr. Gomez nodded, but didn't smile. He looked severe—or sad, I didn't know which. "You go along and finish your breakfast," he said. "Your uncle and I have something to discuss."

As Wolf and I walked away I heard their voices, but I couldn't make out what they were saying. I was fairly sure, though, that the "something" they were discussing was the beast Schmidt and the way he was treating Wolf.

I glanced down at Wolf who was trotting beside me. "He's a monster," I said aloud. At which point Wolf wagged his tail and leaped around. I was glad to see that the whiplash across his face had not touched his eye, but it had left a small cut down the middle of his forehead.

"We'll take care of that when we get in," I said, and went straight from the front hall upstairs, where I put some disinfectant on the cut. Wolf wasn't crazy about that, and he whimpered a bit, but sat like a soldier throughout.

When we went down to finish breakfast, Paul was there. His face and eyelids were a little puffy, and he barely grunted when I came in.

"Hi," I said, and slid into my seat. Wolf sat down beside my chair. There was a little bacon left on my plate, and I slipped it to him. He gobbled it up, and then put his front paws on my lap, his long nose groping towards the plate.

"HEEL!" Paul roared, stood up and came around, his napkin raised as though he were going to use it on Wolf.

"Heel yourself!" I said, jumping up. "Wolf is now mine, and I'm not going to have him yelled at and abused."

"Yeah, I bet," Paul said, trying to push me aside. "That dog's got to learn manners."

There was a low growl behind me.

"Paul, sit down at once!" Uncle Brace was standing in

the door. As Paul turned, he started coming in. "Wolf has been given to Hilda by Mr. Gomez. He is her dog, and he is not to be disciplined by anyone else. Do you understand?"

"Oh, all right." Paul sat down. "She'll ruin him, of course."

"No, I won't," I said.

"In any case," Uncle Brace said, "he is hers to do with as she wishes."

"Schmidt won't be happy about that. He's guaranteed—"

"We will not discuss it further," Uncle Brace said, his voice like steel.

Paul shrugged.

I knew I should hold my tongue, but I couldn't help it. I said, "And considering how sloshed you were last night, I'm not sure you're the one to talk about discipline."

Paul's muddy gray tan flushed red. "That's got nothing to do with it. You wouldn't understand. Men have to—"

"That's enough," Uncle Brace said, and then, his eyes going past Paul, "My dear, you should not have tried to come down. You know you must rest."

Aunt Louisa, supported by Williams, was making her slow way into the dining room. "Thank you," she said, as Williams gently lowered her into her chair. "I thought I should at least be here for Hilda's first breakfast." And she gave me a smile so distant that it was as though it had nothing to do with me.

"Williams," Uncle Brace said, "you will see to it that Mrs. Kingsmark will return to her room immediately after breakfast."

"Of course, sir."

"I think I'll have a muffin," Aunt Louisa said almost dreamily. "Williams, will you go and ask Cook to toast a muffin for me?"

"But Mr. Kingsmark told me—"

"At once, Williams."

Aunt Louisa's tone surprised me. She sounded as though she knew what she was asking, and why, and meant to be obeyed. In other words, as though she were aware of what was going on, instead of in her usual fog.

I watched the iron gray maid hesitate, then leave the dining room.

"Come and sit beside me," Aunt Louisa said to me.

I got up willingly and walked to the other end of the dining table, followed by Wolf.

She regarded him with some wariness. "I thought Brace wouldn't allow animals in the house."

"Mr. Gomez said he was to be mine, so it's all right this time. He's very friendly. In fact, that's what got him into trouble." I was speaking in a low voice, hoping that my aunt and I could have a private conversation. I wished the two men, Uncle Brace and Paul, would talk to one another. But Paul was sullenly finishing up his bacon and eggs, and Uncle Brace was sipping his coffee, staring straight ahead. If his ears had waved like the Elephant Child's I could not have been more aware of his listening.

"Hilda," My aunt said. "You must—"

"Here you are," Williams' flat tone cut across whatever Aunt Louisa was about to say. "Luckily Cook was already toasting one of these so-called English muffins. There's nothing English about them if you ask me."

"But we didn't ask you," Aunt Louisa said. "Now why don't you run along upstairs and iron my blue dress for me?"

"Rosa's done that, Ma'am. I'll just wait here until you're ready to go up again."

I prayed silently that Aunt Louisa would send her away the way she did before. For a moment I thought she might.

She raised her eyes and looked at me for a moment, and it was the first time I felt that we were really looking at one another. Always before it was as though I were staring into a fuzzy wall. But then she lowered her eyes again, and I knew she didn't have the strength to try again.

I got up. "I think I'll take Wolf for a walk," I said.

"Excellent," Mr. Gomez said, entering the room. "May I have the pleasure of going with you?"

For a second I hesitated. I wanted so much to be alone. But he was the one who had rescued Wolf and had said I was to have him. "Of course," I said.

"Tell me about yourself," Mr. Gomez said.

We'd been walking on one of the paths going through the jungle, and the heat was stifling. No air could get to us.

"It's hot," I said. "Isn't there any way on the island where we could walk out in the open?"

"We're heading towards the main road that goes around the island. When we hit that, it will be more open and we will get the breeze. It's only a short distance now."

But it seemed longer. The trees and undergrowth on either side of the path were so thick, and the trees so tall that they created the impression of a tunnel. I could hardly breathe, and I kept slapping away at my legs. "The mosquitoes here are terrible." I glanced at his arms below the roll of his shirtsleeves. The arms were strong and sinewy and tanned, and didn't look like an old man's arms at all. "They don't seem to bother you."

"To some extent, we build up some kind of immunity. Our blood smells less attractive, or something. Newcomers like yourself have a bad time, I'm afraid. By the way, did you have any shots before coming down here?"

"What kinds of shots?"

"Typhoid. Tetanus." He stopped on the road. "I thought

45

Louisa mentioned them in her letter to your . . . to Mr. and Mrs. Tashoff.''

"Well, nobody said anything about it to me.''

"I see. Well, that should be remedied.''

At that point the narrow road turned right, and in front of us stretched a wide expanse of tarmac, a rim of trees, and the head of the cliff. On the other side of that, from where we stood, was only sky. I took a deep breath. "That's better. It's stifling away from the breeze.''

Wolf obviously felt the same way, because he ran across the road, stood looking over the cliff, ran a few yards up, then back and barked excitedly.

"Yes, all right," I said, "we're coming.''

"I didn't thank you properly for him," I said as we turned right and started walking up towards the high point of the island. "I'm so glad to have him. I've never had a pet, because Mother's allergic, but I've always wanted one. And I think Wolf is terrific.''

He looked sideways down at me and smiled. "What will your mother do about her allergy when you show up with him?''

"She'll just have to get shots or something. Other people do.''

He glanced down at me for a moment. "Perhaps you would like to come and visit me in Brazil—on your way home, I mean.''

"I couldn't do that. But thanks.''

"Why not? Would your parents mind? After all, they didn't mind your coming down here to visit your Aunt Louisa and Uncle Brace. And there would be no extra expense, of course.''

"You mean you'd pay?''

"It would be my pleasure.''

"Why—why do you want me to visit you?'' I asked.

"We hardly know each other." And I looked up at him. His face had strong, fine bones, and his nose in profile was slightly aquiline. As that thought touched my mind it also touched something in my memory.

He was looking down at me. "What is it?" he asked.

"Nothing. Just . . . just something about you reminds me of something, but I'm not sure—I can't think—what it is."

He surprised me then, by touching my cheek with his fingers. I thought, I wish he were my uncle instead of that awful Uncle Brace.

"Perhaps it will come back to you," he said.

4

"What do you mean? Come back to me?" I was suddenly aware that my heart was beating faster, and that I was upset. But I didn't know why.

He took his hand away. "Whatever it is that you want to remember, but can't." His brows were up, his tone dry. He suddenly looked like what he was, an austere, aging man named John Gomez. He was obviously elderly, his hair was gray, the skin around his eyes and beneath his chin was wrinkled. Yet he looked younger than some of my father's friends.

We walked in silence for a while, Wolf running ahead, sniffing at every stone and tree trunk, then turning back, to make sure we were there.

"That man's a sadist," I broke out suddenly. "Beating Wolf like that. He'd have to be. Wolf's such a super dog. I don't believe that's necessary for training at all. But when I think of what the other dogs here must go through—"

"Your uncle tells me that he—Schmidt—is perfectly all right except when he's drinking. That his discipline of the dogs is restrained and that he is good to them. Unfortunately, not too often, he drinks. And when he gets a dog that defies him—"

"He has no *right* to abuse another creature. *None.* My father—"

"Yes," Mr. Gomez said after I'd paused. "Your father?"

"He's a fanatic about people's rights, all creatures' rights."

"You're fond of him."

It wasn't a question, yet I felt I wanted to answer. "I think he's wonderful. Just before I came here, he was, well, distracted, I guess. I'm sure it's because of the new book he's involved with." And when did I decide that, I wondered. I'd told myself that before but I knew better. He'd been distracted, often, when he was working on a new book project, but never from me. All of a sudden I remembered his putting his hands on my shoulders, and then withdrawing.

"Something is upsetting you?" Mr. Gomez asked, but I didn't answer.

We walked for a few minutes. I threw a stick for Wolf, who went tearing after it and proudly brought it back in his mouth. "Good dog," I said, and patted him.

"Do you enjoy school?" Mr. Gomez asked.

"Yes. Of course, it's a drag sometimes, particularly with subjects I don't like. But most of the time it's great."

"What subjects don't you like?"

"Algebra. I hate all those equations."

"Does your . . . your father help you with them? Or your mother?"

"No. Father helps me with things like history and political science. He hates math as much as I do. Mother ought to like it, since she's a medical technician, but she says she hated the mathematical part, too. So I'm on my own, and sometimes it's a little dicey whether I get a 'C' or something worse."

"What do you want to be when you grow up?"

"Well, I always thought I'd go into publishing or something like that, like my father. But just lately, in fact, just now, I was wondering if I'd like to be a vet."

He smiled down at me. "You'll have to struggle with some of those hated formulas if you do. Vets have much the same training as doctors, and chemistry, which has a lot to do with formulas, is important there."

"Yes. I know. I guess I'll have to get coaching."

"I suppose it would seem strange to you if I said that mathematics has its own beauty—not unlike poetry."

"You're right," I said. "It would." I realized that sounded rude. "I mean, I'm not saying it's impossible. Just that I can't imagine it." I looked at him for a minute. "Are you a mathematician?"

"I started out to be. At least, I started out to become a physicist, and physics has a great deal to do with pure mathematics. . . ." He paused.

"Why didn't you go on?"

He hesitated. Then he smiled. "Let us say that life intervened."

I smiled back. There was something terribly nice about him. Especially about his face, which both bothered and attracted me. *But he's old,* I told myself. Hastily I said, "My father has a friend who says 'Life is what happens when we make other plans.' "

His laugh rang out then, and for a moment I had an idea of what he must have been like when he was young. Then he put his arm around me, grasping my shoulder. "I must remember that. It's wonderful!"

For a moment I felt strangely close. Then I moved away. He's just a dirty old man, I thought. And with that thought came another. I've got to get out of here.

50

"Come on, Wolf," I yelled. And then said, "I ought to be getting back."

He didn't say anything. Just stood there.

It was several days later that Paul drove me down one afternoon to the small village to have the shots that I was supposed to have had before I flew out here.

When Paul and I hit the coast road to the village I was struck again with the island's incredible beauty. "It makes me think of a Rousseau painting," I said.

"What does?"

"The island. There are so many greens." And there were: the fresh green of the hillsides where the trees had been cut back, the green of the lawn in front of the house and the green of the vegetation and the trees. It was a landscape of greens dotted here and there with a brilliant red of some kind of plant.

"What's that red plant over there?" I asked.

"Hibiscus."

We drove for a while. The Jeep rounded a curve. "Here's the village."

To me, a village had always meant two streets and a green, New England style. Here there was a square. On opposite sides were pink, white, yellow and blue adobe houses, with a frame house dotted here and there, also painted in one of the common pastels. On a third side was a white stone building with wings and arches and next to it a surprisingly large church with a steeple. Opposite was a long, low whitewashed building which, from the red cross on the white flag in front, I took to be a hospital. The sidewalks of the square were filled with people, ranging from white through tan, brown and black. All—both men and women—wore large straw hats and were either looking in shop windows or standing in bunches, talking. Mostly the men wore white, and the women wore dresses, skirts and blouses of pastel cotton.

We drew up at the hospital. "The doctor's office is in here," Paul said. "Brace has already talked about the shot or shots you're supposed to have, so you don't have to explain anything. I'll pick you up in an hour. I've got to go to the post office to get the mail and get on the two-way radio to fix up that tennis party."

That reminded me of something. "Uncle Brace said there wasn't a phone, but that man, a servant, came and told him he was wanted on the phone. Why did he lie?"

"He didn't. It's not a regular phone, but a line to his main offices around the world. Don't ask me why he has that and why the other phones don't work. I'm not an electrical engineer, and I don't know. See you later."

A receptionist sitting in the front hall of the hospital told me where the doctor's office was.

There was no air conditioning in the hospital, although the air in the town was a lot hotter than up at the house. The famous Maenad wind could be felt more easily at the higher points on the island. But the halls in the hospital were amazingly cool, and every few feet there were huge ceiling fans keeping the air moving.

The doctor's offices were on the ground floor, and the waiting room was filled with people. Before I saw them I could hear their voices, light and cheerful and often full of laughter from down the hall. But when I opened the door and came in the talking ceased. Faces turned towards me. I stood in the door there a moment, shocked by the sudden silence, and the people and I stared at each other. As I looked I had a sudden, incredibly clear vision of heads withdrawing into windows, pulling shutters after them, closing out the enemy. It was as clear as a series of photographs. Then the pictures vanished. Those in the waiting room turned their heads away. Some looked down, others stared straight ahead. There was hardly a sound. At the other end of the room a regular nurse in a white uniform sat. She stood up and came towards me. "You are Miss Kingsmark," she said.

"No. I'm not." The strength of my denial startled even me.

"You are not? But Mr. Kingsmark said—"

"My name is Tashoff. I'm Hilda Tashoff. Mr. . . . Mrs. Kingsmark is my mother's cousin."

"Oh."

There was a slight noise behind me. I turned. A pair of dark eyes were staring at me with an unreadable expression. The woman who was looking at me was large and heavy. On her head was a kerchief of the same print as her skirt. Her features were strong and I had an impression of a magnetic and dominating personality. Then the eyes dropped. The tension in the room was like a string being drawn.

"Sit down, please," the nurse said.

There wasn't an empty seat anywhere. "I'll just stand here," I said, and stood with my back to the door. As I stared ahead, I wished I had brought a book or a magazine to read. I also thought that, allowing for half an hour, or even twenty minutes, per patient, I'd be there until the afternoon. Suddenly I was aware that one of the other women was speaking to me. Not much older than I, she'd stood up. "Miss wish to sit down?" she asked.

"No, that's fine. I don't mind standing." I was horrified. Why should she offer me her seat? I could imagine my father's outrage at all the possible implications.

She glanced down at the older woman sitting next to her. Something, whether a glance or a muttered word I couldn't be sure, passed between them.

"Miss sit down," the girl said, moving away from the bench.

"No thanks. Really."

"Sit down!" This time the words came from the woman in the kerchief across from the girl. It was an order. I stiffened. Much as I didn't like the class or racial distinctions implied by the girl's offer of her seat, I also didn't like being ordered around. "I prefer to stand," I said.

I don't know what would have happened if the inner door had not opened at that point. A middle-aged woman came out, laughing, followed by an elderly man. He looked around the room and caught sight of me. The smile faded from his face. "Ah, Miss Kingsmark."

"My name is Tashoff," I said firmly. "Hilda Tashoff."

"But you are of Mr. Kingsmark's family. Mr. Kingsmark called us."

"I am a cousin—a distant cousin—of Mrs. Kingsmark."

"Ah," he said. "Mrs. Kingsmark. I see." The silence that had existed before he came out of the office, spread again. What is the matter with all these people, I thought. Except that that didn't feel like the right question. It would better have been put, what is the matter with me?

"Come into my office, please. Your uncle said you needed some injections."

I opened my mouth to say, he is not my uncle, he's married to my aunt. But it seemed surly. "All these people were ahead of me," I said instead.

"Please come in, nevertheless. It will only take a moment." And he went back into his office. I hesitated for a moment, then followed him.

It was a small room, not overly clean. Dust was on the venetian blinds and the doctor's ashtray was full of cigarette ends. On the other hand, his sterilizing equipment was steaming away, and he was reaching into it with forceps to get out a syringe.

"I'm going to give you booster tetanus and one shot of typhoid," he said. "You can have the second in a month, here or at home. You should have had them before you came. I'm surprised your doctor didn't realize that. Or your mother. You live in Brazil?"

"No. I live in New York."

"Oh, I thought . . . Well, roll up your sleeve."

The needle plunged in and was removed. He swabbed the faint prick, threw away that needle, attached another ampule and needle, and gave me the second injection. "Well, there are your tetanus and your typhoid. You shouldn't have any trouble. If you do, let me know. And here's your prescription for the malaria pills. You should have started them a couple of weeks before you came, of course. Just as you should have had the shots before you left the States. I'm surprised your . . . your uncle and aunt didn't write you."

"I think Aunt Louisa forgot."

He looked up at me for a moment. "Very likely," he said finally and lowered his head. After a final squiggle he handed me the prescription. "You can get that filled in the dispensary, it's at the other end of this corridor. Take a tablet immediately, and then after that, once a week." He got up suddenly. "That's all."

"Why did you take me ahead of the others?" I blurted out as I rolled down my shirt sleeve.

He gave me a strange look. "On this island, Kingsmarks always come first."

"Do . . . does Uncle Brace own this island?"

"Legally, no. In effect, yes. And all who walk here. Now if you'll excuse me, some of those outside have been waiting awhile."

"I didn't ask you to take me first."

"No, but if I had kept you waiting, sooner or later I would have heard about it. Good-bye."

I wanted to ask what he meant, but he was already showing another patient into his office.

The encounter with the doctor was depressing, and the twenty minutes in the waiting room among the silent, hostile women was . . . frightening, although when I tried to arrive at the reason why I found it scary, I couldn't come up with an answer. But I was extremely glad to be out of the doctor's offices and was quite determined not to go back, no matter what happened. But then nothing was going to happen, I told myself.

I picked up the malaria pills at the dispensary and left the hospital. Paul and his Jeep were nowhere in sight, so I decided to walk around the square. As I stepped out of the colonnade, the heat hit my face like a burning fan. I had my dark glasses with me, but they protected only my eyes, not my face and head. As I hesitated, I could see across the square a shop with big straw hats similar to those worn by the women in the doctor's waiting room piled outside. What I needed was one of those.

To get there I passed first in front of an official-looking building which seemed to be a sort of town hall, and then the church. The church walls were whitewashed a blazing white and the light seemed to radiate from the walls. Pausing, I stared up the few steps leading to the entrance, but all I could see was the dark of the interior. On an impulse, I went up the steps and walked inside which, by contrast to the sidewalks and the square, was deliciously cool. But it was so dark after the sunlit street that I could see nothing except the banks of candles and, up at the other end, an enormous crucifix. There were pews in the middle, but the rest of the marble floor was bare, except for the women who knelt on the floor. There were others in the pews, many with rosaries dangling from their hands.

I had had no religious upbringing whatsoever. My father was a nonpracticing Jew, and my mother a nonpracticing Episcopalian. I considered myself simply nonpracticing, a nonbeliever.

I stared at the bent figures, wondering what they were feeling. My parents were the kindest people I knew, yet I also knew that my father would have described what I was looking at as superstition in action, and my mother would have called it a peasant church, and then apologized for sounding snobbish. Thinking about it, I grinned.

"Do you find the religious practices of the natives amusing?" a voice said in English just behind me.

I swung around, and my heart gave a funny jump. There was Steve Barrington, the pilot of the plane. Somehow he seemed different, and then I realized why. "What happened to your mustache?" I asked. He was clean-shaven and looked much younger.

"I shaved it off. I have to go to Boston to see somebody at a college there, and thought I'd better look less piratical."

"Are you going to school in Boston?"

"I applied there. As well as Columbia. They want to see me."

"Terrific! What are you going to take?"

He hesitated. "Eventually, medicine."

"You're going to be a doctor?"

"That's the general idea. Back to my original question. Why were you smiling, unless, as I suggested, you found our customs quaint?"

"I was smiling because I was imagining something my parents would say."

"What?" He had on jeans and a shirt with the sleeves rolled up and seemed taller than I remembered.

"Well, Father'd call this—" I waved my arm over the church, "superstition. He's nonreligious Jewish. Mother would call it a peasant church. And then would feel guilty for having sounded snobbish."

He laughed. "And what were you brought up as?"

"Nothing. What about you?"

"Well, my parents came out to Sibyl from England. But I was brought up in a church like this. Mother was Irish and therefore Catholic."

"Oh. I thought you were a native."

"I am a native. A native of Sibyl, that is. I was born there." He grinned. "You know the rule. If you're born in an oven, then you're a biscuit."

I giggled. "You're right."

"How do you like Maenad?"

For a few seconds I'd forgotten about my uncle and aunt, about the huge house and Schmidt outside beating the dogs, and my aunt with her strange, spaced-out gaze and the women at the doctor's office. Now it all came rushing back. "If you want the truth, not much."

"Why not? Aren't your relations showing you a good time?"

"Oh Steve, they're . . . they're strange."

He didn't say anything for a moment, then, "Well, I could have told you that."

"What do you mean?"

He didn't answer for a second. Then, "Tell me what you mean, first. Then I'll tell you what I mean. Let's go have a soda or something."

"I'd love to, but . . . but Paul Kingsmark is supposed to pick me up in the Jeep."

"He'll see us. Don't worry. We're just going to the little café outside the hotel."

The hotel was in the middle of the next block. It was

hardly your average neighborhood Hilton. In fact, I wouldn't have noticed it at all until I was right under a small sign saying "The Maenad Inn." Like the church, its front was whitewashed, and tucked into one of its walls, under a canopy, was an area containing about six small tables.

We sat down and a waiter came over. "Hello, Tony. Let's have a . . ." Steve glanced at me.

"Coke," I said.

"And a ginger beer. Now," he said, when the waiter drew a lazy rag over the table and then went off to get our orders. "What, in particular, is strange about your rich relatives?"

"I hadn't realized they were that rich," I said. "It was sort of a shock."

"They could hardly live in that house with umpteen servants if they weren't. Or fly their private plane."

"I didn't know they had a private plane."

"They have two in their hangar near the field, although I suspect that one at least belongs to Gomez."

"Mother and Father didn't tell me anything about their being so rich."

"Didn't you tell me she's a very remote cousin of your mother's?"

"Yes." Something was struggling up in my memory.

"Maybe your mother didn't know."

"She said, I remember now, something about that side of the family always having more money. But I didn't take it to mean rich, as in private planes and dozens of servants."

Steve grinned. "Aside from their conspicuous consumption, what else do you find strange about them?"

I hesitated, wondering where to begin, wondering how I could make him understand my overwhelming sense of alienation from everything they seemed to represent.

"Well, for one thing," I said finally. "Aunt Louisa.

She's so weird—she practically looks through me when she says things but seems to be thinking about something else. And that grim female that hovers around her—Uncle Brace is always ordering her to take Aunt Louisa upstairs, or something.''

"Well, I can throw a little light on that. Anyone on the island could. Your Aunt Louisa is a drug addict, and has been for some time."

5

For a moment I simply stared at him.

"Hey!" he said. "I didn't mean to knock you flat. I'm surprised you didn't know it yourself. Anybody who's ever been around addicts would know it. I suppose you haven't been."

I shook my head.

"You knew she was strange. What did you think was the matter with her?"

"I suppose I thought there was something wrong with her—mentally, I mean."

"You could say that there is. But it's been induced by drugs."

"How *horrible*." Somehow, because Aunt Louisa reminded me of my mother that made it worse. "How . . . how did it happen? I mean, everybody knows that the jet set's always sniffing cocaine—you can read it in the papers. But I've always thought it meant people like rock singers or movie stars."

"And not your respectable corporation wife."

"No."

"Well . . ." Steve stared down into his drink.

I waited, and then, when he continued to be silent I said, "Well, what?"

"What I'm going to repeat to you is only island gossip, and it's not very flattering to . . . to your uncle."

"He's not my uncle!" I countered, with more vigor than I'd intended.

"Okay." Steve grinned a little. "For what it's worth, the gossip is that your . . . your non-Uncle Brace got his first money by marrying your aunt, and when she started not liking some of the things he did, he gave her pills to calm her down. And that was the beginning."

"What sort of things?"

"I can't really be definite about that."

I looked at him, and knew that there was something he was not telling me. "Steve, please tell me what you're . . . you're holding back. I know there's something."

"There's nothing I have any definite knowledge of. Truly. Just a lot of talk and suspicions. But that's to be expected where there's one ruling family and everybody else on a different level. I mean it's not as though there was a county or country club set. It's the Kingsmarks and—at their level—that's all. If they were all saints, there'd still be gossip, because in a confined area, gossip makes life more interesting. To add to that, every now and then one of their blasted dogs gets out and does a lot of damage. So that makes the family even less well-liked."

My head came up at that. "You mean the dogs they train?"

"Yes. They're killers, some of them."

"Wolf's not a killer."

"Who's Wolf?"

I told him all about Wolf. "He's simply wonderful—affectionate, gentle, not a bit like the others, at least, if the others are the way you say." And as I spoke I had a sudden vision of the man Schmidt—his face red, his eyes glittering with an ugly light. Couldn't any dog beaten by him become vicious? "There's a man named Schmidt," I started.

"Yes, indeed. He's well known. He drinks a lot, and when he's drunk, he's inclined to stagger down to the square here with one or two of his dogs, let them off the leash, and then almost die laughing when they terrorize and harass any people who're in the park. If I were you, I'd keep your pet out at the house until you go back to New York. But I'd be damned sure before then that your Wolf has escaped whatever strain in those dogs that makes them so mean."

"Wouldn't you be mean if you were beaten? It doesn't follow that they're born that way."

"I had a strong impression that they were deliberately bred to hold and increase that vicious streak, but you may be right, it may be more nurture than nature. I still think you oughtn't to let your friend off the leash down here. There are plenty of natives who'd be delighted to kill any of those dogs on sight, if they thought they could get away with it."

"I certainly won't bring him down here." I sat there and once again felt bewilderment and anger that Mother should have let me come to such a place without finding out about it, regardless of how much she might consider Aunt Louisa "family."

"How long are you staying here?" Steve asked.

"Not long, I hope. Paul's gone to get the mail, and I'm hoping there'll be a letter for me saying how soon I can come home. Daddy went to do some research in South America, and Mummy went with him. My sister Juliet is in camp, so the apartment's closed up."

"Where in South America?"

"I'm not sure. Brazil, I think."

"Ummm. That's where Gomez comes from, isn't it?"

"Yes," I said, surprised. "I hadn't thought of that."

"Had you met him before? Is he related?"

"Good heavens, no. Why on earth did you ask that?"

"Nothing. No reason. Well, here comes your Jeep."

I turned. Paul was parking the Jeep, a scowl on his face. Then he sat there, waiting, obviously expecting me to come up.

Out of sheer cussedness I decided he could come over and collect me.

"Your chauffeur is waiting," Steve said.

"I know. I think I'm going to wait until he comes and announces he's here officially."

"I take it you don't much like him."

"Not a lot. He's a drag. He also gets drunk, and I think that's really gross."

Steve laughed. "I'll see who's going to win this."

"I am," I said, hoping I sounded a lot surer than I felt. But I reassured myself that even though he went off and left me, I had Steve, who would take me up to the big house.

"Don't look at him," I said. "Pretend we don't know he's there."

"That's going to take a lot of make-believe. But I'm willing to give it the old college try. And apart from all that, Mrs. Lincoln, what did you think of the play?"

I giggled.

"Don't tell me you haven't heard that before."

"Yes, but it sounded funnier when you said it."

"It's either my magic charm, or the circumstances. I suspect the latter, unfortunately."

"Don't put yourself down. I'm enthralled."

"Yes, you look it. I've never seen anyone work so hard not to notice someone. However, I'm bound to say that I think it's working. Your friend Paul is climbing out of the Jeep and stamping over here. Not at all pleased."

"All right, Hilda, let's go," Paul said, sounding extremely cross.

"Oh, Paul," I exclaimed, as if I hadn't had an idea he was around. "I want you to meet Steve Barrington."

"We've met," Paul said briefly. "Hello Barrington."

"Hello Kingsmark. What are you so angry about?"

"Nothing important. Are you ready, Hilda? We're supposed to be back up at the house."

"What for?" I asked, as innocently as I could. "It's not as though there were a crowd with lots of plans."

"As it happens, there is going to be a crowd, coming over from Sibyl in a day or two, and there's a lot that has to be done."

I knew absolutely that there was nothing for us—Paul and me—to do. Whatever had to be done would be done by the servants. But it confirmed my suspicion that Paul was angry to find me talking to Steve.

"Is there any mail for me?" I asked.

"No. You've only been here a couple of days. Why should you be expecting any mail?"

"Because either Mom or Dad always writes to me." The disappointment was, I knew, disproportionate. I didn't always get a letter from the family this soon when I was away. Nevertheless the fact that I hadn't received one increased my uneasiness.

"Well, they're probably too busy checking out South America. Come on, now."

Slowly I got up. "Steve?" I started. I wanted to ask him where I could keep in touch with him—he seemed the one sane person in a very crazy island world. But I didn't want to ask in front of Paul.

Steve got up, too. "It's been great seeing you." He put out his hand and I clasped it. "I'll be in touch," he said, and tightened his clasp for a moment.

"We're going to be pretty busy," Paul said.

"Never too busy for friends," I shot back, delighted at Steve's gripping my hand like that.

"You can't tell." Paul spoke with increasing surliness. "And the people up there—your aunt and uncle," he added for emphasis, "can be choosy about who they invite."

"You know, Paul," I said. "You ought to put in for a brand new set of manners." I turned to Steve. "Thanks. I'll look forward to hearing from you." Then I went and got in the Jeep.

We drove in silence for a while, and drove fast. When we got out onto the road through the fields, chickens and ducks and a couple of dogs sped out of the way. When we nearly hit a cat I said, "Paul, slow down. Do you have to take your bad temper out in nearly killing things?"

"We're late for tea," he said, but he did slow a little.

"I don't care whether I have tea or not. And I'd a lot rather not have tea than kill some helpless cat or chicken."

"They'll all land in the pot anyway."

"Surely not the cat."

He shrugged. "Who knows."

"Are you angry because I was having a drink with Steve?"

"I told you, he's a native. And the Kingsmarks don't hobnob with the natives much."

"I find that kind of discrimination disgusting. I can imagine what my father would think of that!"

"Your father—that's a joke!"

"What do you mean by that?"

"Nothing—forget it!"

"I'm certainly not going to forget it. What on earth made you say that?"

Silence.

"Paul, if you don't answer me, I'm going to tell Uncle

Brace what you said, and ask him what he thinks you meant by that." Truthfully, I thought Paul was simply being unpleasant, but I didn't think he should get away with it.

"That's very funny, you don't know how funny! You just go ahead and do that and then tell me what he says." And Paul started to laugh, weaving the racing Jeep from one side of the road to another as we avoided more wildlife.

I was both angry and scared, scared because the road was full of potholes and the Jeep swayed unpleasantly from time to time. From the smell of his breath, I was fairly sure Paul had had one or two drinks for the road and I didn't think he was in any shape to decide what was merely stupid from what was dangerous. But I was not going to give him the satisfaction of appearing frightened.

"I will do that," I said. "As soon as we get back." It gave me some pleasure to notice that Paul slowed down as soon as we came in sight of the house.

"Well," Mr. Gomez said, as we sat at tea. "Did you get your shots?"

"Yes. And some malaria pills."

"It's always a good idea to be careful." And then, "Paul tells me that a group of young people are coming over tomorrow to play tennis and swim. That should be fun for you."

I stared at Paul sitting across the room next to Uncle Brace. Aunt Louisa was, as usual, sitting behind the beautiful teapot, her eyes moving slowly, and with a faintly bewildered expression to the face of whoever was speaking. For a moment, and because there was a resemblance between them, Mother's face seemed superimposed over her cousin's. The contrast between the vacuous stare of the woman in front of me, and my clear memory of Mother's lively, highly expressive features, was overwhelming. *Your Aunt Louisa is a drug addict, and has been for some time.*

"Is everything all right?" Mr. Gomez said beside me.

I turned and looked at him. Of the four of them—himself, Uncle Brace, Aunt Louisa and Paul—he seemed the most normal, the most sympathetic. "No, yes," I said. And then added, "I have to talk to Uncle Brace."

"Anything I can do? You uncle is sometimes a little pre-occupied. He has much on his mind."

I looked into the calm, clear blue eyes and felt an impulse of trust. "Well, all right. But . . . maybe not now."

"We could have a walk after tea. Take Wolf with us."

"Yes. I'd like that. But I'm going to keep Wolf on a leash if we go anywhere near any other house, or the village."

"The village would be a long walk, but we can certainly take a leash with us. Are you afraid he'll do something?"

"Steve said," I started, and was aware that Paul, who had been staring in his teacup, raised his head.

"Yes, do tell us what your pilot friend said," he sneered.

"He said that the island natives hated and feared the dogs, because sometimes Schmidt would get drunk, go down to the village and let dogs off his leash to harass the people there. He said that plenty of natives would kill any dog that got out on sight."

"That's an absolute lie," Uncle Brace said, his face red.

"No, I don't think it is." Mr. Gomez' steady voice stopped him. "I've seen Schmidt. He should not be allowed near animals. I've seen him drunk and we are all aware of what he tried to do to Wolf."

"He likes hurting things," Aunt Louisa said in her dreamy voice.

"You are hardly a reliable observer, my dear," Uncle Brace said.

"I may be drugged, but I can see things."

68

There was a silence. ''You must get rid of Schmidt,'' Mr. Gomez said. And in the way he said it, I knew that he could give Uncle Brace the order.

''Do you own this house?'' I asked him.

He looked down at me. ''No, your uncle does. But . . . he often follows my advice on such matters.''

''Game, set and match,'' Paul said, and laughed.

''Go to your room!'' Uncle Brace ordered.

Paul got up. ''With pleasure. It's not as though the company down here is enlivening. Hilda here prefers the natives.''

''You will apologize to Hilda,'' Mr. Gomez said. ''At once.''

Paul got white. Then he, like Uncle Brace, flushed. His eyes dropped. ''I'm sorry,'' he muttered, and left.

''And now,'' Mr. Gomez said, rising. ''Let's have that walk.''

''I really don't think,'' Mr. Gomez said, as we entered the tunnel-like path that led to the main coastal road, ''that you have to worry about a leash for Wolf as long as we are with him.''

''No,'' I said. ''And I don't want him to feel . . . tied, trapped. Do you . . . do you think he might develop a . . . a mean streak, later on, the way Steve said?''

''I seriously doubt it. He certainly didn't show any viciousness under extremely harsh circumstances. But, if you care for him, that is a risk you have to take, isn't it?''

''Yes.''

As though aware of the fact that we were talking about him, Wolf came plunging back, jumped up on me, regarded Mr. Gomez politely, and then went back to exploring the path.

''He really is *wonderful*,'' I said.

Mr. Gomez looked down at me and smiled. "When you love, you love."

"Of course. Don't . . . doesn't everybody?"

He didn't answer that, but said, after a minute or so, "You really like this Steve Barrington, don't you?"

"Yes. Is there any reason I shouldn't?" Since I was sure Mr. Gomez would also bring up the fact that Steve was a "native" I spoke rather belligerently.

"None that I know of."

"Paul seems to think that natives are inferior."

"And you don't."

"Of course not. Do you?"

"I don't think the natives are inferior, but I do think that one must think carefully and at length before marrying out of one's own background."

"Well, I wasn't thinking of marriage."

"Weren't you?" He smiled at me again. "When most girls have that star-struck look they are thinking about marriage, however far down the road."

I could feel the blood surge up to my cheeks. "Good heavens, he's not even finished with school yet, and after that he's going to medical school."

"I see."

"Why's Paul so against him?"

"Jealousy, I expect. They're almost the same age, yet Barrington pilots his uncle's planes and seems to be much more of an adult in an adult world."

I paused, then blurted out, "Steve said the whole island knew that Aunt Louisa is a drug addict."

"I could wish your Steve had been a little more . . . discreet. He didn't have to put it to you quite so brutally."

"He didn't. I said she was strange, spaced out, and then he told me that. It's true, isn't it?"

"Yes. But try not to judge her—or Brace—too harshly.

Your uncle tells me her drug addiction started when she had a series of breakdowns and had to be put on powerful antipsychotic drugs. She is, and always has been . . . mentally unstable. After that, well, she drifted into taking other drugs.''

I shivered. "It's horrible."

"You know no one else who takes drugs?"

"No. No one. I mean, living in New York, you hear about it a lot. But I've never known anyone who used them."

"Your . . . parents must be very careful of you."

"What a funny thing to say." I paused. "I suppose they are. I mean, they don't let me go out with anyone they don't know. . . ." Suddenly, and with an odd stab of anxiety, I remembered Paul's sneering reference to Father. "Paul said something, when we were driving back. . . . He was saying how the Kingsmarks didn't hobnob with natives, and I said I thought it was horribly discriminating and I could imagine what my father would think of a statement like that. And he said something like 'Your father—that's a joke!' And when I asked him what he meant, he said, 'Nothing— forget it!' And I said that if he wouldn't tell me, then I'd ask Uncle Brace what Paul meant, and then Paul said I didn't know how funny that was . . . that I was to go ahead and tell him and then tell Paul what Uncle Brace said. . . .''

There was a long silence as we walked. I could hear Wolf scrabbling about in the thick undergrowth and among the trees at the side of the path. Somewhere there was the sound of water flowing or falling . . . and there was an occasional clack or chirp of some bird.

I knew the question I was going to put to Mr. Gomez, but for some reason I was having great difficulty in getting it out. I felt like the man in the legend, pushing the rock up the slope . . . what was his name? We had it in mythology . . . Sisyphus. But I had to ask it . . .

"Do you know what Paul meant?" I finally said.

I was staring down at the path, as though, if the answer came, I wouldn't have to look at it. But the answer didn't come. Instead there was the sound of frantic barking, a yelp, and then more barking, and the noise of undergrowth being trampled.

"Wolf!" I cried. "Wolf!" And plunged after him.

"Come back!" Mr. Gomez roared. "It's not safe there."

But I didn't bother to listen. I could hear the noise going on up ahead. More barking, another yelp. Somebody was doing something to Wolf.

"Wolf!" I yelled again, "Come back here instantly. This minute! Wolf, come back!"

I could hear the feet behind me and knew that Mr. Gomez was coming after me. But I had been a runner for years, and had run in the mini-marathon in Central Park. Even so, running here was dangerous. Vines and creepers covered the path, and branches lay across it.

"Hilda, come back. There are snakes here! You must come back at once!"

I heard him, but pretended I didn't, and put on another burst of speed. "Wolf!" I called again. "Wolf, come back!"

And he did. I broke into a small clearing, and there he was, loping back towards me, a piece of cloth dangling from his teeth.

"Where have you been?" I scolded, while hugging him. "And what's that?" Wolf, proud of himself, had deposited the rather damp piece of white cloth in front of me. "What do you suppose it is?" I asked Mr. Gomez, who had come up behind me.

He took it. "Obviously a piece of clothing, but it could belong to anyone."

"Do you think Wolf was in danger?" I asked anxiously.

"Not unless whoever it was had come here with the idea of killing a dog. After all, this is not that far from the house. If a dog wandered down to the village or to one of the farms, then the chances of its being killed would be much greater."

Another uncomfortable thought hit me. "Do you think he bit someone?" If he had, he'd be in even greater danger.

"I hope not."

"Come on, Wolf, let's go back."

"But we haven't had our walk," Mr. Gomez said reasonably. "Within a few minutes we'll be out on the main coastal drive, and it will be much more open." We stood there, as I hesitated. Then he said, gently, "What are you afraid of?"

"I'm afraid of what might happen to Wolf."

"This Steve seems to have upset you a great deal. I wish he had kept some of his . . . thoughts . . . to himself."

From having been the only one of the four that I really trusted, Mr. Gomez promptly joined the other three in my estimation.

"Steve only answered questions that I asked. And if it's true that some of the dogs have been made vicious—having seen Mr. Schmidt I think it would be strange if they weren't—then I don't blame the people who've been harassed for wanting to kill them. I'd rather know how they felt than take Wolf down there. I'm very grateful to Steve."

That attractive half-smile lifted the corner of his mouth, and he made a funny gesture, striking the heel of his hand against his head. *"Dummkopf!"* he said.

I laughed. I couldn't help it. "What's *dummkopf*?"

"Dummkopf? It means stupid. After talking earnestly to

you about young love, I then criticize the beloved. That is indeed stupid."

"I didn't say I was in love with him."

"You didn't have to."

I laughed.

"Shall we finish our walk?" he asked.

"All right. For a bit. How often does the mail arrive?"

"To the house? As often as someone goes down to the post office to get it. It comes into the village whenever a plane comes. Most of them bring some airmail. But there is no distribution of mail. Why do you ask?"

"I was hoping to get a letter from either Mummy or Daddy. Maybe one will come in . . . well, I suppose it's too late today. Tomorrow."

"But I thought there was a letter for you," he said, and then, as I stared, "perhaps I was mistaken."

I faced him. "What made you think it, then? Did you see it? Did somebody say something?"

"Halt, halt!" he said, laughing. "I am trying to remember."

"Let's go back and see, now. Come on, Wolf!"

We walked back rapidly and in silence. I knew Mr. Gomez was disappointed, but I couldn't help it.

As I ran into the hall I bumped into Uncle Brace. "There was a letter for me, wasn't there?" I burst out.

"A letter? No, there wasn't. If there had been I would have given it to you, of course."

"But Mr. Gomez said he thought he'd seen one." At that point, Mr. Gomez came up the front stairs behind me. "Didn't you?" I said, turning to him.

"Didn't I what?"

"Didn't you say I had a letter from Mummy and Daddy?"

"I thought you did." He glanced at Uncle Brace. "I must have been wrong."

"Sorry to disappoint you," Uncle Brace said. "Maybe the post tomorrow."

I stared at him for a moment, then glanced swiftly at Mr. Gomez.

"Would you like to continue our walk?" he asked.

"No, thanks. I think . . . I think I'll have a bath before dinner. Come on, Wolf!"

"Dogs should not be—" Uncle Brace started.

"But Wolf is different," Mr. Gomez interrupted. "He can go with Hilda anywhere."

"Yes, yes. By all means," Uncle Brace said, as I marched behind Wolf across the hall and up the stairs. I knew I was being abrupt with Mr. Gomez, who was trying to be nice, but my dislike of Uncle Brace had become almost overpowering. By way of contrast, I thought how much I liked Steve, and how I wished he were here now. *"I'll be in touch,"* he said, and I ran the words over in my mind as though they were prayer beads.

But, half undressed, I paused. *How* would he be in touch?

Uncle Brace had said there wasn't an ordinary phone that anyone could use in the house; only a company line. My heart sank. Sitting in the bath, with the water growing rapidly cooler around me and with Wolf happily snoozing on the bath mat, I brooded over that and my growing conviction that there *had* been a letter for me. When the name Tashoff appears on an envelope, I told myself, it would be difficult for anyone to mistake it for Kingsmark or Gomez or . . . Williams, Aunt Louisa's grim maid. Running against this in counterpoint I heard, in my mind, my father's voice, "Hilda, for heaven's sake, don't let your imagination run to melodrama."

His voice was so vivid that, as I stood with the towel

wrapped around me, a wave of homesickness swept over me. What was I doing on this godforsaken island with its weird people (except, of course, Steve) cut off from everyone I knew and liked (except Steve and—I glanced down—Wolf)?

At that moment one of the maids, a young, light brown girl with dark eyes and a pink kerchief around her head, came in the bedroom door. She stopped, flustered at seeing me in the bathroom, standing as though in a reverie with the big towel wrapped around me.

"Oh, sorry! Excuse me, please!" She seemed upset.

"It's all right. Come in." I tucked the end of the towel in under my arm, and came into the bedroom, half closing the bathroom door behind me.

She dropped a little curtsy and came back in and put my laundered and dried underclothes on the bed.

"Thanks. Thanks very much. You shouldn't have done them. I meant to do them but I forgot. . . ."

"No, no," she said. "That's my job. Miss Williams said I was to take care of you. If there's anything you want done . . . your dresses washed and ironed . . . please tell me."

"But you shouldn't be waiting on me. I can do it all perfectly well."

"Oh, no, miss! Please. Do not do that." She spoke in a careful, yet singsong way. "Miss Williams would be most unpleased. She would be cross."

"Why on earth should she be cross just because I do my own laundry?"

"Please miss! Leave it for me. It is better that way." The expressive dark eyes held an unmistakable plea.

"All right. I'll do it the way you want. Don't worry!" Without thinking, I put my hand out and touched the light brown arm.

Her smile was tentative and then flashed like a light over her face. "Yes, miss."

"What's your name?"

"Carlotta."

"Well . . . thanks, Carlotta."

"Thank you, miss." She bobbed another little curtsy and was about to leave when Wolf came out of the bathroom carrying my large, pet sponge.

"Wolf," I said, "have you been chewing my sponge? Bad dog!"

He dropped the sponge at my feet and looked towards Carlotta, ears up, tail wagging.

"Isn't he—" I started, and turned around.

Carlotta was standing with her back to the wall, her face now gray, her eyes wide with terror.

"Carlotta—don't look like that. He's fine. He's not at all vicious!"

Tail waving, Wolf made a tentative step forward.

Carlotta gave a smothered cry and turned towards the wall.

"Carlotta, look!" I said. "He's quite gentle." I had my fingers through his collar and was stroking him. "Please—do look!"

Slowly she turned back.

"Put your hand out—just hold it out like this." And I closed my fist so that the back of my hand was towards Wolf's nose. "He won't hurt you—I promise."

Carlotta was looking at me strangely. "Do you not know these dogs are trained to kill people who are not white?"

"That's ridiculous!" I said. "They're trained as guard dogs for . . . for well, factories and police and search parties and so on."

"That is what they say. We do not believe it."

"But—" And then I remembered Schmidt and his

flushed, brutal face, and what Steve had said about his coming to the town drunk and letting the dogs loose. "Look," I said, worrying again about my pet, "Wolf's only a puppy. He's just nine months old." I leaned down and kissed him on the head and he licked my face. "Please trust him, and . . . and tell everyone else to trust him. I don't want him . . . I don't want him killed."

She looked at me gravely. "Then do not take him down into the town, or anywhere, except up here at the high point."

"But you can see he's harmless. Please put your hand out."

She stared at Wolf for a while. I had put my fingers back inside his collar. However much I wanted to show how gentle he was, I knew that I must not let him loose to go over to Carlotta without her permission. "Sit, Wolf!" I said, without the slightest hope that he would obey. But he did.

"I will not put my hand out," she said finally. "But I will believe what you say." Quickly she bobbed another curtsy and was gone.

Later that night, lying in bed, I suddenly remembered that Mr. Gomez had never answered my question as to what Paul meant by his cryptic references to my father. I had gone over the lines in my mind, so I knew them by heart.

Me: *"I find that kind of discrimination disgusting. I can imagine what my father would think of that."*

"Your father—that's a joke!"

"What do you mean by that?"

"Nothing—forget it!"

"I'm certainly not going to forget it. What on earth made you say that?" And then, *"If you don't answer, I'm going to tell Uncle Brace what you said. . . ."*

*"That's very funny. . . . You don't know how funny. . . .
You just go ahead and tell me what he says. . . ."*

And the memory of Paul's mocking laugh again rang and
jeered in my ears as I lay awake, unable to sleep.

Suddenly, as though it were a cool hand on my head, I realized I had come to a decision: I would go home. Where I
would stay until my parents got back I didn't know. Maybe
with a friend . . . maybe at school, where there'd be a
custodian, at least, and possibly one of the teachers. Nothing mattered except leaving.

It was as though my whole life hung on that . . . as
though something deep within me knew that by staying I'd
be in danger.

The decision must have been the right one, because once
I'd made it, the voices in my head faded and I went to sleep.

6

But the decision had to be postponed. Plans for the young people from Sibyl to come to Maenad had been going forward. Two mornings later they started arriving shortly after nine. They came in four Jeeps, one driven by Paul and the others by some of the male servants.

The moment they got out, laughing and calling to one another, I realized the word "young" could mean a variety of ages. As far as I could judge these were in their very late teens or early twenties, a couple of them even thirty. From Uncle Brace and Aunt Louisa's point of view, they were undoubtedly "young." But from mine, they were another generation.

They came up the steps carrying airline or tote bags.

"You must be Hilda," the first, an attractive girl of about twenty, said, holding out her hand. "Paul and Brace have been telling us about your arrival and we've been looking forward to it. By the way, my name is Rachel."

"Hi," I said, shaking her hand. "Do you live on Sibyl?" It was a stupid question, but I couldn't think of what else to say.

"Yes. You must come over and visit us."

"I'd love to," I replied fervently. Getting to Sibyl would

be one important step nearer home. And from Sibyl planes
left for the other islands and the States.

"We'll fix something up," Rachel said politely. But I
could see she was a little startled by the eagerness of my reply.

The others were all introduced to me. There were twelve
in all, six men and six women. Among the men and the other
women there were no Americans, only Europeans and South
Americans. Rachel, I was sure, came from the States, until a
chance remark revealed that she came from Vancouver.
Why I found this fact slightly depressing I wasn't sure. I had
never been in the slightest bit xenophobic, and our apartment in New York was often filled with guests of other na-
tionalities. But no matter how much I argued with myself, I
couldn't get away from the realization that I had hoped that
at least one person from Sibyl would be a compatriot who
might be willing to help me get home. All the people from
Sibyl spoke English fluently, but they came from various
South American countries, from England and from conti-
nental Europe. None of them seemed to be the kind of person to whom I could say, "I feel trapped. Please help me get
off the island."

The morning seemed to move on treacle feet. I knew the
young crowd had been brought for my benefit, and I knew I
ought to be grateful. Volleying with them, playing a doubles
or singles game, listening to them talk about people they
knew and events they had shared, I made halfhearted at-
tempts to join in. But, the truth was, I felt more isolated than
ever. And the more isolated I felt, the harder it became to
make the most ordinary comment.

Luckily, I was kept so busy my silence wasn't too notice-
able. Those who at any given time were not playing tennis
were swimming, or trail riding, or lying in deck chairs beside the pool. Sometime just before noon two bay horses and

one gray horse had been brought out from stables behind and beyond the house, and Rachel and one of the older men called Clark and I put on jeans, mounted the horses and ducked into the bridle path hidden among the trees.

For a while we rode abreast, in silence. The other two had taken the bays, and I had the gray. "What's his name?" I had asked the groom who was holding the rein.

"Pronto," he said.

Pronto was a tall pony rather than a horse and was smaller than the two bigger bays. Talking to Rachel and Clark, who rode on my left, I had to look up.

"Are you having a good time?" Rachel asked. I glanced at her quickly. "I mean here on Maenad," she said.

For a second I had a wild impulse to say, "No, I feel alone and isolated and I want to go home." But it not only seemed rude—I wouldn't have minded that so much. It seemed babyish.

"Yes, thanks," I said politely. "It's . . . it's an interesting place."

"That is an almost British understatement," Clark said.

I was jolted. Maybe I wasn't alone in my reaction to Tradewinds and to the Kingsmarks. "What do you mean?" I asked.

He looked at me and smiled a little. "When you said interesting did you mean strange?"

"Yes. But I didn't . . . I didn't realize that other people found it as . . . weird as I do."

"It's out of the last century. There are, of course and unfortunately, places like this—setups like this—in South America. But nowhere else in the Western world I can think of." And as I continued to look doubtful, "It's a medieval fief—one ruling class and all the rest peasants—or the Caribbean equivalent thereof."

"Come on, Clark," Rachel said. "You're talking about our hosts."

"Yes. It's bad manners, and I shouldn't. Sorry." He reached up and pulled a leaf from the tree branch sweeping down in front of him.

I was furious with Rachel for stopping him. I knew he felt about the Kingsmarks—certainly Uncle Brace—as I did. But if Rachel thought it was rude of *him*, a casual guest, to comment, what would she think of me if I really said what I felt?

I was still puzzling about this when Rachel's horse gave a sudden neigh, bucked a little and sprang forward. "I have to go after her," Clark yelled over his shoulder at me, as he took off in pursuit.

The bridle path was roomy and fairly straight. But a hundred or so yards ahead it veered, and because thick trees lined either side, it was impossible to see beyond the turn, so both Clark and Rachel disappeared in a few seconds. Pronto had shown modest signs of wanting to run in pursuit, but I brought him to a stop and sat there for a moment or two. After all, Rachel's horse taking off like that was not entirely surprising: Clark had dropped back and was riding a little behind Rachel. From the corner of my eye I had seen his hand, holding his crop, snake out and strike Rachel's mount on his backside. It didn't take a massive brain to deduce that Clark wanted to be alone with Rachel, however much I thought his method stupid and unkind.

After a minute or two I dropped the rein and said, "Okay, Pronto, let's canter." When I reached the turn in the bridle path, I saw a fork about a hundred yards further on. Since the path was at least partly dirt, it was easy to see which path the other horses had taken, and I decided to take the other one.

We cantered on that, and I started to enjoy myself for the first time since I had been to the island.

"All right, Pronto," I said, after a long, exhilarating canter. "We can trot."

Somebody must have loved riding, I decided, because the path veered and turned and forked from one side of the island to the other, covering miles in what was not too large an area. Pronto had an easy canter and trot and was soon promoted to being my second favorite on the island (Wolf being the first).

Except for the clop, clop of Pronto's hooves, the silence that I had experienced before when I was walking with Mr. Gomez lay over everything like a mantle. After a while I slowed Pronto to a walk, and, when we came to a small break in the trees, I got off, tied his reins above his neck, and lay down on the grass and fern and undergrowth. The powerful rays of the sun were filtered through leaves and branches and palm fronds, and I lay squinting up into the dappled light, more at peace than I had been since I had arrived.

I knew I should find my way back to the house, that I should join in more fun and games with the guests invited for my benefit, that everybody would soon be eating a picnic lunch . . . but I wasn't hungry and preferred being alone, and . . . and . . . slowly my eyes closed.

I was back in the house, only not a part of the house that I had ever seen before. For one thing, I was in a deep basement which, in my dream, I knew to be many feet beneath ground level. I was frantic to get out. But every door I tried was either locked, or it opened into another corridor. I knew if I didn't get out soon, something terrible would happen, but I also knew that with every new hallway I went into, I was getting farther and farther away from any stairs or door up to freedom. Then I realized that what I had lost was my freedom, and without freedom I knew I would never find out who I was.

I ran and ran and ran. Somewhere I would find the door leading to the stairs, and behind that door was the person I had always known myself to be, but couldn't now remember. . . . And then the dream changed into my old nightmare, and I was running after the tall shadowy figure because if I could just reach him, everything would be all right. I cried out, but he didn't hear me and I was falling downstairs into a terrible black void. . . .

Something woke me. I sat up and saw Pronto's head up, his ears forward. But whatever had waked me and startled the horse was now silent. I watched his ears twitch.

"Let's go, Pronto," I whispered. Common sense told me that whatever it was I heard was most probably someone—or a group—trying to find me. But however logical, the explanation didn't account for why, quite suddenly, I felt afraid.

Quickly I got on Pronto's back. For a moment I hesitated. If I went back the way I came, and remembered the turning, I'd probably find myself at Tradewinds before too long. Which was where I ought to be. But, after a moment's hesitation, I turned Pronto's head in the opposite direction and took off at a trot.

My parents, I knew, would consider what I was doing the height of rudeness. Guests and a luncheon were all being offered for my benefit, and here I was, doing everything I could to stay away.

But then, why hadn't my parents written to me? Why had they sent me to this awful island among these alien and somehow threatening people without so much as a letter from them? Juliet and I had always accepted the fact that Mother loved to travel with Father, and that he equally wanted to have her along. In a city where half the parents of the kids we knew were divorced, such middle-aged fidelity and obvious preference for one another's company seemed freakish. But it was one of the things that made them nice. Now, when I felt deserted and angry, it didn't seem so nice. It seemed—uncaring. It was at that point that I realized my vision was being impeded by the tears that all of a sudden were rolling down my face. So I slowed Pronto to a walk while I mopped up.

But perhaps they *had* written to me, and for reasons I couldn't imagine, I had not been given the letter. . . . I didn't know whether that made me feel better or worse. For them not to have written meant something that I found frightening and dismaying because of all sorts of implications about the relationship between us and about all my assumptions about them as people. That was worse.

Frightening in a different but more immediate way was the thought that Uncle Brace and Aunt Louisa wanted to keep me incommunicado. No, I thought, not Aunt Louisa, she was too drugged and too frightened herself. If Uncle Brace had an accomplice in this it would be somebody like the grim Mrs. Williams—or Mr. Gomez. But my mind rejected the thought that Mr. Gomez could have anything to do with it. He seemed as straight and honest as anyone I had ever known. And he was the one who insisted that I have Wolf and who agreed that the trainer, Schmidt, was a bullying menace who should not have anything to do with animals. But, all that being the case, it was strange that he was such good friends with Uncle Brace Kingsmark.

By this time Pronto was walking the bridle paths that, I realized, were much narrower than they had been. Also . . . I stopped Pronto and sniffed the air. There was a moist warmth down here, different from the cooler, airier paths and walks nearer the house. Of course, the breeze was stronger up there. It could be felt here, too, but barely. A sting on my arm made me aware that without the constantly blowing wind, mosquitoes and flies were also more plentiful here. Pronto was being bothered by them also. He was tossing his head and switching his tail.

"Okay, Pronto, let's go back and face the music." I wheeled him around and started to retrace our steps. But going back turned out to be a lot more confusing than my pleasant heedless wandering down here. The earth here was harder, the trees thicker, cutting off more light, so that when we came to a fork I couldn't always make out which path we'd come from. After a few minutes, and facing another fork, I stopped Pronto again. Somewhere we had gone completely off. I knew I had never seen either path before.

Perhaps it was because Pronto and I were both so still. Whatever the reason, one minute I was frightened because I was alone in the forest. The next moment I became convinced I was not alone. Off to the left, out of sight behind the trees and undergrowth, there were sounds. Something or someone was moving around.

As I became aware of the sweat that suddenly sprang out on my body I took hold of my courage and called out, "Who's there?" The words sounded eerie among the trees. There were so many trees, so many hiding places. The sounds stopped, and there was silence. Suddenly Pronto reared and something went past my arm. Then there was the sound of footsteps plunging away from us through the vegetation. When I finally managed to calm the horse, I glanced around on the ground to see if there was a rock or something else that someone had thrown. But the hard black dirt was bare. It was only as I was looking up that I saw it. There, embedded in a tree, was a dart. I wasn't about to dismount, since Pronto, if he took fright again, would take off without me. So I walked him over to the tree, leaned over, and pulled the dart out. It was not easy, and I knew the tip of the dart had broken in the tree. But finally I pulled it loose and looked at it. The shaft was thin and long. At one end it was winged with feathers. At the other it was some kind of arrowhead made of stone, and the base of the stone head slanted back to thin points, one of which I had broken off. Even though the front point was embedded in the tree, I could see it had been liberally smeared with something.

There was a pocket at the side of the saddle. I wrapped the arrow in some tissue and placed it in the pocket.

"Okay, Pronto," I said. "Home."

This time, instead of using the reins to guide him, I kept my hands lowered and the reins slack, so that when I dug him with my knees he would go but would choose his own way. To my surprise, he took off down the left path. I knew that my sense of direction was by now zero, but nevertheless, I would have chosen the right—perhaps because the arrow had come from the left. But I had decided to leave it to Pronto, and I didn't stop him. Picking up the reins, I urged him to a trot. We had been traveling only about five or six minutes when we came to something I had not seen anywhere before near the bridle path. On the left of our path was a clearing, with a hut, a fire on a rough tripod in front, and some children playing. Without thinking, I slowed. The children were suddenly quiet, standing, looking at me and the horse. Then a woman came out of the hut, and I recognized her from the doctor's waiting room—she was the one who had ordered me to sit down. Out here, she seemed even larger and more dominant, and I could tell she knew I had recognized her. Pronto had stopped, and she and I stared at each other.

"What are you doing down here?" she said. Her voice was clear, her diction perfect, though she spoke with the island accent. But there was a leaden quality to her words.

"I got lost," I said.

"It is not wise for you to be here alone. You must go

back. Tell your . . . your uncle that you should not go out alone.'' There was a jeering note to her voice.

''I'm not used to being told whether or not I can go out alone or not alone,'' I said, letting my anger show, not only at the woman and her rudeness and hostility, but at everyone on the island.

''Then go back to where you came from, little lady. People here do not do what they wish.''

At that point, a small child, a little boy in shorts, ran out of the hut with something white in his hand.

''Horsey,'' he said, and ran towards Pronto. I saw that he was holding a cube of sugar. Pronto whinnied. The little boy laughed.

I was thinking what a nice gesture it was when, at that moment, the woman moved. She was incredibly swift for someone of her bulk. The sugar cube was six inches from Pronto's thrusting, eager mouth when the woman yanked the little boy back.

''Give me that!'' she said, and took it from him. Then she looked up at me. ''Now go!''

I dug my knees into Pronto and he broke first into a fast trot and then a canter. I was feeling sick as I adjusted myself to his smooth pace. There had been a strange yellowish tint to the piece of sugar, the same color as the substance on the arrow now resting in the saddlebag.

By the method of letting Pronto choose his own way, we got back to the house in another twenty minutes. The bridle path widened, the air became cooler and clearer, the trees no longer closed off the sky, and suddenly we broke through a path into the open field in front of the house and the courts and the swimming pool.

I had a swift glance of almost everyone in riding clothes and a great many horses, all grouped on the terrace in front of the house. Then someone—Paul I think—yelled, "There she is!" And everyone turned around.

I cantered Pronto up the path by the courts and up onto the terrace.

"Where on earth have you been?" Paul said. "Do you realize everybody up here has been looking for you?"

"Do you know what time it is?" That was Uncle Brace. He did not raise his voice, but it carried an undertone of icy anger.

"What happened to you, Hilda? Do you realize how inconsiderate you have been?" Mr. Gomez' voice was not as cutting as Uncle Brace's. But the tone was not one I had ever heard from him before.

The chorus of angry reproaches had a strange effect on me. The first thing I had planned to do was blurt out the story of the dart and the sugar cube. But for some reason I didn't say anything about them.

"I'm sorry," I said coldly. "I got lost. After all, I don't know the island as you do."

"But we sent you out with two companions."

I looked at Rachel, and a vivid blush went over her face. Somehow I knew she had not told Uncle Brace how I happened to be left alone. But I was too angry myself to care. "Did you tell them how I happened to be left alone?" I asked.

Clark said hastily, "Of course. Rachel's horse shied and took off and I had to follow. When I finally got Rachel's horse to stop, you were nowhere in sight. We waited for you nearly half an hour but you never showed up."

"That's not quite the way you told it to us," Mr. Gomez said quietly. "You implied that Hilda hung back and got lost when you were busy in conversation with Rachel."

"And he didn't tell you that the reason Rachel's horse took off was because he whacked its behind with his crop."

"That's not—" Clark started. His accent was very slight, and I had no idea where he came from.

"Yes it is, Clark," Rachel said, "Mr. Kingsmark, what Hilda is saying is true. I'm sorry."

"And you're right, I didn't pursue you," I said, with my eyes still on Clark, "but I assumed you two wanted to be alone." I turned then, and said, "Thanks, Rachel." I noticed then, for the first time, that she wore an engagement ring.

"All right," Uncle Brace said. His voice had lost its cutting edge. "Of course with all this we haven't had lunch, so let's go in. Hilda, let Pierre take your horse."

I got off as one of the grooms came up to me. "He's a good horse," I said, patting him. "I like him."

Pierre's smile showed in his dark face. "Yes, he is. He is my favorite of all."

Mr. Gomez came up. In his riding breeches and boots, with a light khaki jacket, he looked even handsomer and younger than before. And rather military.

"I'm sorry, Hilda, for having misjudged you. I should have known that something like that had happened."

"Well," I said, feeling less defensive, "if they're engaged, I suppose it's only natural for them to want to be alone."

He frowned. His eyes were very blue under the dark brows. "What makes you think they're engaged?"

"Rachel had on an engagement ring."

"Yes," Mr. Gomez said drily. "But I don't think it's Clark she's engaged to."

"Oh."

After lunch we were all sitting by the pool and I found myself in the deck chair next to Rachel. Even in her bikini she had on her engagement ring. "Thanks again," I said to her, "for helping me out."

"It's all right," she said. And then, noticing my eyes going to her ring, "It's not Clark I'm engaged to. That's . . . well, that's part of the problem."

"Well, if you don't want to marry the person you're engaged to, why don't you get unengaged? I mean, being engaged isn't like being married."

"It is when money and family and property are all locked in."

This reminded me of all the things Father said he was against: people marrying for any reason except what he considered the right ones—mutual love, respect and trust. "We were supposed to have left all that marriage contract and landed stuff back in the old countries," he had once said. How awful to have a father who wasn't like that. I glanced at Rachel.

"You mean your family wants you to marry for money—or property? I think that's *medieval*."

"Well . . ." She looked a little uncomfortable. "I guess it isn't all my family's fault. My father and my fiancé's father are heads of different corporations in the same industry. If we married and the firms merged, everyone would be better off. And even I thought it would be a good idea at the time. But I haven't seen Juan for nearly a year. . . ." She glanced at me. "A girl can get lonely."

Maybe, I thought, she wasn't any more a victim of a wicked father than of her own desire for a little fling.

"You look awfully disapproving," she said. "You're not a bit like Paul."

"That's fine with me. I don't like him."

She shrugged. "He hasn't had an easy time, either. His father, Brace Kingsmark's brother, was stuffy and uptight and proper—something of the old Prussian school. He wouldn't make Paul legitimate until just before he died. So Paul didn't know who he was for most of his life."

"You mean he was illegitimate?"

"Yes."

"Who was his mother?"

"Glamorous and aspiring, but a nobody from nowhere."

I stared at her, feeling my anger grow. "Nobody is a nobody from nowhere."

Rachel gave me a sour grin. "That's one way of looking at it. But not the Koenigsmark—or Kingsmark, if you want the English version—way of looking at things. They have nobility and titles going back to Brunnhilde and Wotan, for all I can make out. The trouble is, all that is back in East Germany, so the family left after the war and settled in South America."

"Poor Paul." For the first time I felt sympathy for him. "Where did he spend most of his time?"

"In schools, both in England and America, paid for by his father."

"But you'd think, with that sort of misery in his life, not knowing who or what he was, and having his mother looked down on, he'd be a radical or something."

"The other way of coping with that is to join the enemy, become more Catholic than the Pope, out-Nazi the Nazis. You know," she continued as I stared, "be so gung-ho that nobody ever looks to see what's behind you."

"So the Kingsmarks are Nazis," I said, with a certain amount of satisfaction. I felt justified in my dislike.

"I didn't say that," she said, alarmed. "And please don't go around saying I did."

"I'm not. Of course I wouldn't say you said that."

"And anyway, it's not true. Not all Germans were Nazis. Some of them are very nice. My fiancé, Juan—his last name is Mueller. He's really Johann Mueller, but his family's been in Uruguay for a long time."

"But I thought you didn't like him," I burst out, tactlessly.

She went bright red. "I do like him. I never said I didn't. I just . . . well, like I said. He's been away a long time. And anyway, who are you to come over so virtuous and pure? You're nothing but a kid. And what have the Kingsmarks done to you, except try and be nice to you? They set up this whole party, but you seem to be the only person not enjoying it. I'll admit running off from you wasn't very nice, but you could have gone back, instead of giving everybody the fright of their lives by staying out and wandering around." And she got up, picked up her sun oil and towel and moved to a deck chair several yards down the side of the pool.

After she'd gone I remembered that she had saved me from trouble by forcing Clark to admit they ran away from me, and then backing me up when I said Clark had whacked her horse.

I got up and went over. "I'm sorry, Rachel. I shouldn't have said what I did. You stuck up for me and I forgot that."

She didn't look at me for a moment, then turned and stared up. "It's okay. But my mother was German, and it always makes me mad when everyone assumes that Nazi and German mean the same thing. Especially," she said drily, "when the people you're talking about were either not born until long after the war, like Paul, or were small children when the war was over, like Brace Kingsmark. In case you didn't recognize it, that's prejudice."

For a minute I couldn't believe what I had heard. After all, to be prejudiced was considered, in my household, the ultimate sin.

"That's funnier than you realize," I said slowly. "My father, who is Jewish, is a great fighter against prejudice. He's written articles and edited books on the subject."

"Well, ask him what he thinks." She hesitated for a moment. I sat down on the pool edge beside her. "I don't particularly like Brace Kingsmark," she went on. "And I sometimes wonder what he's up to. But I like his wife, or I have, on the few occasions when she's been around and well."

"Stephen—" I said, and stopped. Then I went on, "The pilot who brought me here."

"I know Steve. Everybody knows him. His uncle owns the airline and Steve sometimes flies for him. What about him?"

I was astonished at the flash of jealousy that went through me. I'd never felt that before. I looked at Rachel. She might be engaged to one man and flirting with another, but she was attractive and about Steve's age. "Do you know Steve well?"

"Like I said, he's flown some of the planes I have ridden in. He's a bright boy, good-looking, too." Slowly she grinned a little. "You like him, don't you?"

My cheeks felt hot, and I wished I hadn't brought him up. But I had, so I said, "Yes, I do," almost defiantly. And then, because I couldn't help it, "Do you?"

"Do you mean have he and I been out or anything?"

I nodded.

Her grin grew. "I'm terribly tempted to say yes, we went out and made hot love under the palms, just to see your face. But the answer is, no. I haven't been out with him."

I desperately wanted to know whether he'd *asked* her out or not, but was determined not to show my feelings that much. So I glued my lips together and said nothing.

"You were about to say something about Steve, or quote him or something. You said, 'Stephen—' and then stopped. What was it?"

For a moment I couldn't think. Then I said, "Oh,

Stephen said that all the island, this island, I think he meant, knew that Aunt Louisa was . . . had a problem with drugs.''

"I should think that this entire end of the Caribbean knew that. Gossip travels, you know.''

"Mr. Gomez . . . Mr. Gomez said that it was because she'd been ill, some kind of mental or emotional illness, and that she'd become hooked then.''

"It sounds reasonable. Haven't you known people who've had to take the antipsychotic drugs to survive, but have suffered some of the side effects? I have. I can think of a couple on Sibyl.''

"I'm sure,'' I blurted out, "that if Mother and Father had known about her condition—what this whole place is like, for that matter—they'd never have sent me. But the way Mother described Maenad and the house here, it sounded like some super summer house up in Maine or in the Bahamas. I *know* they wouldn't have sent me if they'd known what it was really like.''

There was a long silence. Then Rachel said, "If you hate it so much, why don't you go home?''

"Because Mother and Father are traveling and the apartment's shut up and my sister's in camp. At least that's been the reason until now, but last night I made up my mind that I was going back to New York even if it meant I had to stay with a friend or at school or something.''

"But surely school—if it's a day school—is shut for the summer.''

"There's usually a teacher there. Anyway, I'd find someplace. The problem is getting out of here.''

At that point, Mr. Gomez strolled past the other side of the pool and waved. Rachel waved back, and after a moment I did. He looked hesitant for a moment, then walked off towards the house.

"Now there's an antidote for your prejudice," Rachel said. "He's German, and I think he's terrific."

"But his name is Gomez. That's Spanish."

"Well, the Spanish and the Germans have the same habit of sometimes hyphenating their names with their mother's names. So that he could be Gomez von Himmelbutton or something, but calls himself Gomez. I'm sure he's German. Somebody—maybe Paul—told me."

The moment she told me I was sure, too. Quite why, I didn't know. There was a reason that for the moment I couldn't locate. But the thought of his being German depressed me, which simply proved how right Rachel was about my prejudice.

After Mr. Gomez had gone, Rachel stretched and said, "I can't give you much comfort about leaving here unless you can get your uncle and aunt's cooperation. Planes land only with their permission. There's no other way out of here. Have you any reason to think they'd stop you from going?"

I'd been dry and cool, but suddenly sweat broke out on my body. Without any proof, I was quite sure Uncle Brace would stop me from leaving.

"I'm sure he doesn't want me to go. I haven't actually asked him. But . . ."

"But he gives that impression?"

I nodded. "Yes."

"Well—" She sat up and started rubbing more oil on her already tanned arms. "You can always ask him straight out. But if you do . . . and he refuses, then it might be harder to get away without his knowing."

"But I can't think *why* he wants to have me here. It doesn't make any sense. And not hearing from Mother and Father hasn't helped."

"Haven't they written?"

"Uncle Brace says no. Mr. Gomez thought he saw a letter

for me, but says he must have been mistaken. And they say there's no phone, only a company line. Yet I've heard it ring, and the servants have come to announce that so and so is on the phone."

"Have you looked for it?"

"Not properly."

"Then I would look. There probably is one, and you could call somebody you knew in the States and get them to set up the arrangement to come and get you. Although, of course—" She stopped.

"Although what?"

"If, for reasons I can't imagine, your Uncle Brace doesn't want anyone to land here, he can stop them."

"How?"

"Well, for one thing, by turning off the landing lights on the airstrip, and if that wasn't enough, by putting stuff—cars and station wagons and horses and I don't know what all on the landing strip. But what I can't figure out, is why should he?"

"I don't know. But—" I didn't want to admit it, but it was important to speak the truth now. "I'm afraid of him."

She got up. "Lots of people are afraid of him. My future father-in-law says Brace Kingsmark is one of the most ruthless men he's ever met. If he wants something, he gets it—whatever the cost in whatever coin and no matter who pays." She started to walk towards the house, and I saw that Clark had just come out, and was looking at her.

"Rachel," I said.

She turned. "What?"

"Can you help me?"

She didn't answer for a moment. Then, "I'll think about it. Helping you do something your Uncle Brace doesn't want you to do, could be dangerous for me, and for Clark. Clark desperately needs a job, and he's going to go to work for a corporation that your Uncle Brace sits on the board of. While I'm thinking, you ought to be thinking, too. I think you ought to figure out what it is that your Uncle Brace wants so badly that requires you to be here.''

Eventually, they all went home. Dinner was rather quiet. Aunt Louisa wasn't even there, Paul looked sulky, and Uncle Brace grim.

"Did you have a good time, Hilda?" Mr. Gomez said, and all at once I knew why I believed Rachel when she said he was German, not Spanish. There had been enough Europeans visiting us in New York for me to know that his accent, when speaking English, was German, or at least Teutonic. Theoretically he could have been Scandinavian or Dutch. But he wasn't Spanish. Realizing this had the effect of making me group him with Uncle Brace in trying to deceive me.

"Mr. Gomez asked you a question, Hilda," Uncle Brace said sharply.

"Sorry." For a moment I hesitated on the edge of confronting him with the fact that I wanted to go home. But there was something about the three men at the table, all looking at me, that made me decide to postpone it. It might be cowardice, but I felt I would have a better chance taking my uncle on one-to-one. And I would make a final attempt to talk to Aunt Louisa. . . . I saw Uncle Brace start to open his mouth and said quickly to Mr. Gomez, "I mostly had a good time, thank you. I didn't like getting lost in the forest, which was *not* my fault, but I liked Rachel, and riding was fun. Can I ride anytime, or only when people come?''

"Of course you can ride anytime," Mr. Gomez said. That odd, half-smile touched his mouth. "I thought you rode very well. You must ride in New York." He was trying very hard to be nice, I thought, almost solicitous, as though he wanted to please me.

"Yes. As much as I can," I said.

"Where do you ride?" Paul asked, and poured himself some more wine. I saw Uncle Brace's narrow eyes on him and, remembering what Rachel had said, felt sorry for him. "In Central Park?" Paul went on, swallowing some wine. "I thought the place was thick with muggers."

"Well, they're not trying to mug horses," I replied. "And I have ridden there. But mostly I ride in West-chester."

"Do you have a horse?" Mr. Gomez asked.

"No. I'm trying to save for one."

The blood went up in Mr. Gomez' face, as though something had pleased him. "You should have your own horse," he said.

"Well, that's what I keep telling Father. But he seems to see the horse as a symbol of the rich and arrogant. Mother and I are trying to talk him out of that."

"You know, I expect you would enjoy enormously being on a ranch, with plentiful horses and beautiful country-side."

"Yes, I'd like it a lot. I've halfway planned to go to Jackson Hole, Wyoming, for a summer before college. There's lots of wonderful country there, and lots of ranches."

"Wyoming is beautiful," Mr. Gomez said. I knew from

the way he said it that it was not Wyoming he'd been talking about.

"Have you been there?" I asked.

"Yes. Twice. You are right. It is one of the great beauty spots of the world. The mountains—they march down the valley like so—" and he made a gesture with his hand. "And they go straight up, from the valley floor—no foothills, no nothing."

"The Tetons," Paul said. "They're named for women's breasts." And he laughed.

"That's enough," Uncle Brace snapped.

"But it's true," I said. "They were named by the same French explorers who named La Roche Jaune, the Yellowstone, and one of the ranges there, the Gros Ventres—the big stomachs."

"I don't know where the French get the reputation for being romantic," Mr. Gomez said. "They're very practical—and earthy."

Paul opened his mouth, caught his uncle's eye, and then closed it.

"What were you going to say, Paul?" I asked. Common sense told me I shouldn't antagonize that Nazi sitting at the head of the table—and no matter what Rachel said, I was convinced Uncle Brace would have been a Nazi if he'd been around before World War II. But I couldn't resist the question.

"Nothing," Paul muttered.

"What kind of horse would you like?" Mr. Gomez asked.

At that moment I realized he was planning to buy me one. How I was so sure I didn't know. But it was as though, for a moment, I could feel his feelings.

"I don't know yet," I said, confused and embarrassed. "Probably nothing special. Just a horse with a nice personality. Like Pronto.'' And then I could have bitten my tongue off, terrified that he would offer Pronto to me.

"You should have a much better horse than Pronto," he said.

And I couldn't say anything. I wanted to stick up for Pronto, but if I did, and Mr. Gomez believed me, then he might give him to me, the way he did Wolf. Why I found this so alarming, I couldn't define to myself. If any of Mother's or Father's brothers or sisters had offered to buy me a horse, or contribute to the money I'd saved, I'd jump up and down. So why?. . . I didn't know. But I did know that the strength of my feeling had something to do with fear. So I said nothing. Finally, after a minute, I asked, "Is Aunt Louisa ill?"

"Yes," Uncle Brace said. "A little under the weather."

Liar, I thought.

"Tell me about some of the horses you've ridden," Mr. Gomez said.

So I did, and the dinner droned to a finish. Paul disappeared immediately afterwards.

"Would you like to play a game of cards?" Mr. Gomez asked. "Or perhaps Scrabble?"

"Yes, all right. That'd be nice." I wanted to keep an eye on Uncle Brace, because I was determined to confront him alone sometime that evening, and it would be easier to know where he was if I was downstairs.

We played Scrabble. I expected to beat Mr. Gomez, without even trying hard. But he beat me by a hundred points in an incredibly short time.

"You're fabulous," I said. "And it isn't even your native language." I had visions of him in his Brazilian *rancho* playing hundreds and hundreds of games of Scrabble. "Who do you play with?"

"Now, no one really, except the occasional guest."

"But every time you put letters down you make about three words going in different directions."

He smiled. "I'll teach you."

"I won't be here long enough really to learn properly," I said firmly. I hadn't meant to say it at all, but the words popped out.

I saw the clear, sea-blue eyes on me. "You are planning to leave?"

What an idiot I was, I thought, to say such a thing. I looked at the thin, high-cheekboned face and thrusting aquiline nose. He was being wonderful to me for reasons I didn't understand. But if he didn't want me to go, I was sure he could be just as formidable as Uncle Brace.

"Why are you looking at me like that?" he asked quietly.

"You remind me of somebody," I said lightly—anything to keep him off any hint of my trying to get away. Yet, when I said it, it became true. "You do," I said wonderingly.

"I remind you of whom?" He had started to place one of his counters on the board. But he sat, holding the little square letter.

Far back, something in my mind moved, but I couldn't grasp what it was.

Suddenly he leaned over and with his other hand grasped mine on the table. "Hilda, don't be afraid. You have nothing to fear. Believe me."

Uncle Brace walked in. "How's the game going?"

Mr. Gomez withdrew his hand and retreated within his formal self.

"Fine," I said. "Mr. Gomez is beating me hollow."

"He's probably the world champion," Uncle Brace said drily. "He defeats everyone hollow, even Louisa. When she was better, she was quite a Scrabble player herself." He pulled a book off one of the shelves. "Well, back to the salt mines. I have to do some long-neglected work."

I waited till he walked out of the room, then I said, hurriedly, "Excuse me," to Mr. Gomez, and ran after him. "Uncle Brace," I called after him. I had debated in my mind asking him my question in front of Mr. Gomez, because the latter had come to my aid in the case of Wolf, and he might again. But at the last minute I decided not to. Mr. Gomez might not be as helpful on the subject of my going home.

He stopped and turned. "Yes?"

"Can I speak to you a minute—privately?"

He stood, working his jaws back and forth a little, rather like bulls I had seen in the country. "All right. Come to my study."

I followed him down the hall, through a door, and then down another long hall. Finally, at the end, we went into a door on the left.

It was a huge room, with far more bookshelves than I had seen in other parts of the house. They rose to the ceiling, beyond a little gallery that ran around the top. Attached to a rail was the same kind of ladder they have in libraries or old bookstores. Across the room was something that looked like a cross between a sideboard and a console. From inside there was a slight click and whirring. On the floor was a dark red carpet. There was a huge table with magazines and newspapers in a variety of languages all over it, a television set, a large desk of polished dark wood in the middle of the room, and over an empty fireplace, a portrait of a man in uniform with a row of medals and what looked like a sword down his side.

"Who's that?" I asked.

"My grandfather."

"That's a grand sort of uniform." I saw, under the man's arm, the helmet with the spike coming out of it. "What country is it?"

"Germany. World War I. What is it you wanted to talk to me about, Hilda?"

I took a breath. "Uncle Brace, I think it's time I went home." I rushed ahead. "I'm very grateful to you and Aunt Louisa, but I really think I should get back."

"But why? You've only been here eight or nine days. We are trying so hard to give you a good time. Have you heard from your parents?"

If he hadn't said that, the meaningless conversation could have waffled on for hours. I didn't think he cared whether I was enjoying myself or not. But when he said, "Have you heard from your parents?" I knew he was needling me.

"No, I haven't, unless there was a letter you didn't tell me about."

"But why should I keep a letter from you? What strange notions you have, Hilda! Are you often bothered with these . . . these fantasies in New York? Of course, you are related to your Aunt Louisa through your mama"—he pronounced it in the European way, with the emphasis on the last syllable, ma*ma*—"and they say such things are genetic." His mouth was smiling, but his eyes were like little black stones. "As I'm sure you've noticed, your Aunt Louisa is not herself much of the time, and this is because of having to take certain drugs to stabilize her mental illness. I would be so sorry to think that you might be going in the same direction as your aunt."

"I'm not," I said, so angry I could hardly think. I knew that in some way he was threatening me, although I couldn't have said exactly how. "It's just that Mr. Gomez thought I had a letter."

"He also said he was mistaken."

At that point the console gave a sort of chirp and started rat-tatting away.

"Excuse me," Uncle Brace said, and walked over,

pulling up the top of the console. Underneath was some kind of a machine with paper coming out of it. Uncle Brace lifted the paper and was in the middle of reading that when a phone started ringing.

"I'm afraid you must excuse me," he said. "We'll talk some other time."

The phone rang again, but I couldn't see any instrument. "Close the door behind you."

I knew perfectly well that if I refused, he'd probably force me out. So I shrugged, "whatever you want," and walked slowly, towards the door. The phone stopped ringing as I reached it, and I could hear Uncle Brace's voice but nothing he was saying, or even whether he was talking English. Just as I left, I looked back. The bottom drawer of the desk was open, with a key still in the lock. The telephone, which had obviously come out of the drawer, was now resting on the desk. Uncle Brace looked up, saw me watching, and made a quick, angry, "go away" gesture. Then he stopped talking into the receiver, and said to me, "You will leave now."

I did, and then hovered on the outside, determined to go back as soon as Uncle Brace had finished talking and ask him to make arrangements for me to return home. I had carefully left the door open, so I could still hear his voice. Leaning against the wall, I stood on one foot and then on the other. Finally I was aware that the voice had stopped, and there was a slight "ping" as though a receiver had been replaced. Without knocking, I went back into the room.

"I told you to leave," Uncle Brace snapped, with no pretence now at being pleasant.

"I didn't come back until I'd heard you'd finished on the telephone you said you didn't have."

"I said I had a company line. And I do. You would not be able to make local or any other calls on this. This is solely for the use of my company, and I employ a password so that the switchboard knows it is I speaking.'' I didn't know whether I believed him or not. But I didn't have time to think about it.

"Uncle Brace, I want you to make arrangements for me to go back to New York.''

"You were invited for a month and have been here only, as I said, eight days. I will let pass the rudeness to me and to your Aunt Louisa, and to our houseguest Mr. Gomez, but your parents said you were coming for at least three weeks, and all our arrangements have been made to accommodate that. No, I will not help you to go home. I don't think your parents are in America now, and I will not be responsible for a young girl like you, without money, wandering around New York trying to find a place to stay. That is all. You may go.''

We stared at one another for a moment. I knew that to talk to him any further was useless. In fact, Rachel had been right: I had probably damaged my case by bringing it up at all. He now knew how much I wanted to go, and would probably watch me accordingly.

"All right,'' I said, hating myself for not telling him what I thought of him and his Nazi methods. But first things first, as my mother was given to saying. And the first thing was to try and get out of here.

I turned and went towards the door.

"And Hilda,'' Uncle Brace's voice was both sharp and strong. "I must ask you not to repeat this conversation to anyone.'' That seemed such an admission of guilt on his part that my heart, perversely, lifted. At least it proved it was not my imagination that was at fault. But I had no more than acknowledged this thought, than my heart sank again. "Especially I do not want you to mention it to Mr. Gomez. He lost his own daughter last year, and one reason we invited him here, was to try and get him out of the depression he was in over it. We didn't plan to have you both here at the same time, but it's turned out a godsend for John Gomez. You are the same age as his daughter, and he told me how much you reminded him of her. You will cause needless pain if you tell him that you wish to go home. Since he has nothing to do with it, it seems a pity. Goodnight now.''

As I walked back along the hall, I decided that Uncle Brace's touching story about Mr. Gomez could be just as easily a lie as the other things he'd said I was sure were lies. He didn't want me to tell Mr. Gomez because he knew the latter might help me.

I walked back into the sitting room. Mr. Gomez was there reading a copy of the London *Times.* He looked up when I came in.

"Did you have a good talk?" he asked, getting up. "Shall we resume our game?"

I didn't answer the first question, and pretended to be examining the letters I had. I wanted to ask my question in as normal and casual a voice as possible so that he wouldn't be on guard.

"I think it's my turn," I said, and started putting a word down on the board.

"That's very good indeed," Mr. Gomez said enthusiastically, as he counted up my score. "You're well ahead now."

I slipped my hand into the bag to get some more letters. "Uncle Brace said you had a daughter once."

I could feel the sudden tension in him from across the table.

"Yes, that is true." He was looking steadily at me from across the table.

"And that . . . that you lost her."

"Yes. I did. Through my own stupid fault." Abruptly he got up, but not before I saw the sudden tears in his eyes. Evidently, Uncle Brace was, for once, telling the truth. It was so unlike the rather soldierly Mr. Gomez to fight tears, that I felt doubly bad. "I'm sorry I mentioned it. Come on back and let's finish our game."

I knew he would let me beat him, and he did. We didn't talk any more. His face looked drawn and tired, and I remembered how old he was, something I often forgot. Right after the game I went up to bed. I, too, was tired, but what was making me tired was the realization of how totally I was trapped.

Perhaps because I was tired, I went to sleep immediately, with Wolf lying on the bed with me. But I woke, abruptly, some time later, with my heart pounding. I had dreamed again that I was in a house from which I was trying frantically to escape but every door and every window that I tried turned out to be locked. Then the dream changed. I was still in a house, but it was a different one. It was low and one-storied and went on and on, and through the windows and the open doors I could see mountains. In this house, I was not trying to get out, but to find something I had lost. In the beginning of the dream I thought I would find it but at the end of the dream I knew I wouldn't and my sense of loss was overwhelming. It was then I woke up. I was terrified—whether of the dream or something I had heard I didn't know.

Putting out my hand I touched Wolf, and could feel the tension in his back. "What's there, Wolf?" I whispered near his ear, and got a wet kiss on the cheek in response.

Then I heard it: a faint, barely audible creak. It was so faint I had no idea how near it was to my door. Just as I was running through my mind all the perfectly ordinary reasons why someone should be in the hall at—I glanced at my illuminated traveling clock—at a quarter to three in the morning, I heard the creak again, louder this time, and nearer to my door.

Quietly I sat up in bed, and kept my fingers hooked through Wolf's collar. If he jumped off the bed, he might be heard, and his nails would certainly make sounds on the wooden floor around the edge of the carpet. There was a high, faint moon, and I could see just enough to make out the outlines of various pieces of furniture. I was braced for seeing my door open, when I heard something entirely different. It sounded halfway between a whimper and a moan. Then it came again, loudly, making the hair stand up on my head.

My feet found my slippers and I yanked the cotton robe off the chair beside my bed. I opened my door as quietly as I could, and was relieved to hear no sound. The hall was dark, but there was a line of light down at the other end, and I slipped out the door, closing it after me so Wolf wouldn't get out. It was while I was standing there beside my own door that I heard the sound again, only louder, and followed this time, with a "Don't, please don't! I don't need it, I don't want it!"

I left my slippers where they were and ran on naked feet to the end of the corridor. The shaft of light came from a door that had not been completely closed. In a few seconds I was peering through the crack.

It was, I could see, Aunt Louisa's room. She was lying in bed, straining away from a hand that was holding a hypodermic.

"No, I don't need it. Not any more. Please, please don't make me!" But at that point the needle plunged down. I could see the body on the bed slowly relax.

Uncle Brace straightened, the syringe still in his hand. Someone else was holding Aunt Louisa, but was hidden from me by a large armchair between me and the bed. Then he moved, and I saw it was Mr. Gomez.

"That should hold her for a while," Uncle Brace said, and started towards the door.

I fled down to my room and slid through just in time, yanking my slippers in with me. From inside, I peered out through the door and saw first Mr. Gomez and then Uncle Brace come out of Aunt Louisa's room. They didn't act as though they heard anything. As they came down the hall I withdrew my head and heard them pass. They didn't stop at my door and I felt fairly sure they didn't know it wasn't quite shut.

After they'd gone I stood there, shivering in the breeze that blew through the windows, lifting the curtains. I thought about Mr. Gomez and our pleasant walks together, about his making Uncle Brace give me Wolf, about his Spanish name and German accent, and now about his involvement in keeping Aunt Louisa drugged. He gave me Wolf, but he held Aunt Louisa while Uncle Brace shot her full of drugs. . . .

Eventually, I went to sleep, but not before I had made up my mind that I was going to get myself off the island somehow, and that my first step towards doing that was to get in touch with Steve Barrington. How I was going to do that I didn't know. Lying there, I cursed my own stupidity: I didn't have Steve's address, other than simply "Sibyl," and I couldn't even remember the name of his uncle's airline. I was fairly sure that if I sent a letter addressed to Steve via "Sibyl Airport" it would probably reach him. But how was I going to mail the letter? Letters to be posted were put on the table in the hall, stamped and ready to go, and sometime during the course of the day they disappeared. I hadn't even inquired how. Probably, I thought now, the person who went to the post office to pick up the mail also took the outgoing letters.

But a letter in my handwriting addressed to Stephen Barrington and left on the table would announce its sender immediately, and I had no faith whatsoever that it would ever reach the post office. Therefore I had to get it there by some other method. I could, of course, ride to the village with whoever took the mail, and pretend I was going for some other reason, such as getting something from the drugstore. And when (and if!) the driver were elsewhere, slip into the post office and drop the letter into the mail slot. There was nothing wrong with that scheme at all, except that I was afraid I had ruined any chance of its working by letting Uncle Brace know how eager I was to go home. Because of that, I was sure he would have me carefully watched. If I were anywhere near the post office I would not be left alone, and if I were, Uncle Brace was quite capable of calling up and finding out to whom I had written. Everything I had seen about him and the island led me to the conviction that, in effect, he owned it and everyone on it; what he asked for, he got. Then I lay there and wondered if I were showing the first signs of terminal paranoia. . . .

Whether I was or not, I finally decided, one thing was certain: Uncle Brace was not stupid, and if he did find out to whom I was writing, he would put two and two together in no time at all, especially as Steve was known all over the island to be his uncle's pilot. Furthermore, I did not think the letter would reach him.

There had to be some other way. I was still trying to figure out what it might be when I fell asleep.

8

No way presented itself to me the next day, and I was never alone to think about it. Aunt Louisa was not at the breakfast table, but Uncle Brace, Mr. Gomez and Paul were all there when I got down, rather later than usual, and it was as though my conversation of the night before with Uncle Brace had never taken place. He and Paul teased me about sleeping late, and Mr. Gomez smiled at me across the table and joined in occasionally as though we were all one big happy family. I went right along, because somewhere in the course of the night I had decided that my greatest hope of escape was to let them think I had abandoned all thought of it. So I made giggly comments back mostly on the theme of a girl needing her beauty sleep, and I thought if my parents had heard five minutes of it, they would have known I was up to something.

But they weren't there, and even to think of them brought pain, as though in some way I knew that they either couldn't—or wouldn't—help me. When I thought of that, behind my giggly face and stupid jokes, I also realized something else: I was angry with my parents, angrier than I had ever been in my life. For reasons I didn't understand and they didn't bother to explain, they had gone off and left me.

Furthermore, I no longer bought the explanation that Mother had been taken in by a wonderful letter from Aunt Louisa, describing this evergreen tropical prison as another and warmer Bar Harbor or Lyford Cay in the Bahamas. Aunt Louisa couldn't have any more written a letter like that than I could write one in Latin. There was something else going on. And whatever it was had to do with that morning when my father had received a letter, after which he had never, to me, been the same.

Curiously, when I woke up and then sat down to breakfast with Uncle Brace, Mr. Gomez and Paul, I didn't know that I knew all this, but at the end of that horrible meal, during which I did some of the best acting of my brief drama career, I knew, or was sure of all of it. How I knew I didn't know either. Whatever had happened to me, had happened in my unconscious, while I was sleeping, and then emerged into my conscious mind while I smiled and laughed and nibbled at a piece of toast and acted as though I was as happy as a flea with a new dog.

"So," Mr. Gomez said, "we will go riding this morning and perhaps will sail this afternoon. Your uncle said he would lend me his sailboat. Have you ever been out sailing, Hilda?"

"Yes, once or twice, when I was staying with friends."

"Did you enjoy it?"

"Well, it was all very new. And I wasn't sure what I was supposed to be doing." In actual fact, I had decided that on a boat you got to know the other people far better than I really ever wanted to know anyone. Sailing, I had decidedly felt, was not for me. Riding yes, jogging yes, tennis yes, hiking yes, climbing yes, sailing no. I never wanted to be anywhere I couldn't get off. However, if my riding and sailing with Mr. Gomez would take everybody off guard, then I would do both, and give every impression of loving it. I smiled and mentally counted how many of my teeth showed.

Mr. Gomez smiled in return. "I will show you what to do on a sailboat, and then you will enjoy it."

A boat, it suddenly occurred to me, was a conveyance. It went across water. How far was Sibyl? Then I thought about sharks, and how much nicer planes were. . . .

For the next several days I rode and swam and sailed and sailed and rode and swam, always with Mr. Gomez. And I forced myself to remember, several times an hour, that he was at least partly responsible for Aunt Louisa's condition. Because it was sometimes hard not to like him. He had a good sense of humor. He was considerate, and he didn't patronize me. But sometimes he surprised me.

"You know," he said, on the third afternoon, "if you had enough experience sailing, you could stop acting and start actually liking it."

"What makes you think I'm acting?" I asked sharply.

He was leaning, his body half off the boat, as he worked with the jib, but he pushed it away and sat back up. "Aren't you?" he asked drily. "It's a good performance. But that's what it is, isn't it?"

For a moment I was tempted to tell him the truth. But I made myself remember his hands holding Aunt Louisa down, while she pleaded with the two men not to drug her. And I also made myself remember again my first object: to escape. So I smiled. "No. It's not."

Things were a bit silent and stiff after that, but we were at the end of our sail, and were occupied with getting the boat into the little cove and tied up to the tiny pier that had been built at the foot of the cliff.

"Hilda," he said, as we got out of the car behind the house. "Please don't be afraid of me. You have no reason. I would not do anything to harm you."

I just said, "Thanks for the sail," and walked up the steps, knowing that he was watching me.

That night when I went to bed I couldn't sleep. Wolf was beside me, as usual, and I stroked his head and ears. Outside I could hear the wind, higher than it had been for a while, whipping the trees. I turned over and tried all the usual methods of sleeping: counting, trying to imagine a peaceful scene, even getting up and doing some yoga exercise I had learned at the Y at home. But although I was desperately tired, I couldn't seem to relax. I knew the reason: I hadn't been able to devise any way to get in touch with Steve, and all my acting was for nothing if I couldn't do that. Was there anyone on the island I could trust? Carlotta's face seemed to appear in my mind. I could ask her to mail a letter for me, but would it get through our local post office? Even more, wouldn't I place her in danger of Uncle Brace's wrath? Thinking of Carlotta made me think of the women in the clearing.

And then, for the first time in four days, I remembered the arrow I had stuck in Pronto's saddlebag. I was so astonished at having forgotten it, that I sat up in bed. Right after Pronto and I got back from that fateful ride, I was indignant at Uncle Brace's anger with me and decided not to mention having an arrow shot at me, and after that the episode had slid from my mind.

Slowly I lay back down in bed. Unless one of the grooms had cleaned out the saddlebag the arrow would still be there, and since I was supposed to go riding with Mr. Gomez in the morning I could easily find out. But who would I ask about it? If I mentioned it to Uncle Brace, he might use it as some kind of excuse to keep me in the house. He might also take it out on some of the local people. And no matter how much I was lulled into thinking well of Mr. Gomez, I had to remember he was hand in handcuff with Uncle Brace, so I couldn't trust him, either. And Aunt Louisa—I didn't even know where she was. Except, of course, that she might be in her room down at the end of the hall, drugged by the grim Williams, or Uncle Brace, or even Mr. Gomez. I glanced at my illuminated clock. It was nearly midnight. It was almost three when I saw the two men forcing a hypodermic needle into her arm. Did that mean that the drug—whatever it was—wore off at night? Everybody who'd ever watched television or read any books knew that drugs wore off. But beyond that, I didn't know anything about them.

Slowly I sat up again in bed and listened. The house was quiet. I could hear nothing. But in a place the size of Tradewinds, that did not mean that people might not be awake somewhere, talking, and about to come up the stairs. After sitting there for a while I decided to risk something. If I were caught, there would be no ordinary excuse I could make. I couldn't say that I had lost my way going to the bathroom, because my bath was through a connecting door to my bedroom. I would just have to say I heard a noise and had gone to investigate, and stick to it.

As on the previous occasion, I put on my robe, but did not put on slippers. Pushing Wolf back, I slipped out of my door and into the dark hall. Then I walked as quickly and calmly as I could to the door at the far end where Aunt Louisa slept. But this time there was no shaft of light to guide me. When I got to the door, I stood, my ear to the keyhole, listening. I could hear nothing. As quietly as I could I turned the doorknob and eased the door open. Except for the pale light of the moon, the room was dark, but Aunt Louisa's bed was in a shaft of moonlight. Before I moved I peered into the murk to see if there were other doors to the room, and I saw two: one of which most likely led to a bathroom. The other was next to her bed, and I had no idea at all where it might go.

And then something happened that made me freeze, my

hair lifting off my neck. Aunt Louisa's voice, dragging but unmistakable, whispered, "Hilda?"

Leaving the door slightly open, I ran across the carpet and knelt by her pillow. "Aunt Louisa?"

"Is it you, child? I can't see."

"Yes, it's me. Why are they doing this to you?"

"Because—but there isn't time to tell you. Any minute Williams or Brace will come in and give me another shot. I've been lying here, praying that you would come, trying to call you in my mind."

"It worked. I wasn't even thinking about it, and then I decided to try. That's *spooky*."

"Where the mind is concerned, things are a lot spookier than people believe. But I don't have any time to tell you . . ." Her voice dragged weakly. "Listen to me. You must get out of here. Brace . . . they plan to take you to Brazil."

"Why? Why? And why did Mother and Father let me come to a place like this?"

"Because of Gomez. He—" And then we both heard: steps in the next room, coming towards the door.

"Get under the bed, quick," she said. "Hurry, hurry!"

I was under the bed, hidden by the ruffle when the door opened and footsteps came across the carpet. One set of footsteps came to stand on one side of the bed, and the other pair went around the foot of the bed and stood on the other side. Squashed under the bed, I tried to breathe as silently as possible.

"Louisa, are you awake?" It was Uncle Brace's voice.

There was no reply, and I knew, as though I were in her mind, that Aunt Louisa was pretending to be unconscious, so that her husband might think she didn't need an additional shot.

"Maybe she doesn't need another injection," he said.

I heard the bed squeak a little, then Williams' voice said,

"She's awake, Mr. Kingsmark. Just pretending that she isn't. Look, I'll show you." There was a brief silence, then a sudden cry from Aunt Louisa.

"You see," Williams said.

"I could have found that out for myself, Williams," Uncle Brace said. "You did not have to jab her with a pin. Why were you pretending to be asleep, Louisa?"

"You know why, Brace." Aunt Louisa's voice was still draggy and very tired. "I don't want you to give me so many injections. I don't need them."

"You pleaded with me to give them to you not too long back. Don't you remember? You said you needed them to stay on balance. And our doctor agreed. And when you changed your mind, and started refusing to take the medicine, you had a very bad breakdown, remember?"

"Yes. I remember. But I don't need this much, and you know I don't. You're keeping me this way so you can do what you want—and what Hans-Gunther wants. And you know if I were well I would stop you somehow."

"Well," Uncle Brace said, and he must have leaned on the bed because it creaked again, "you've answered your own question as to why I keep you in this condition."

"But it's wicked. She's nothing but a child."

"That's the whole point, my dear. And now you must let Williams hold your arm."

"But why, Brace, are you helping him?"

He gave a short, exasperated sound. "As though we hadn't discussed this ad nauseam. What about our indebtedness to him? Williams, hold Mrs. Kingsmark's arm ready."

I heard a slight sound, then nothing. Then, after a few minutes, a long sigh.

"That'll hold her," Uncle Brace said.

Williams asked a question that sent my heart to my knees. "Would you like me to sit on watch here?"

If Uncle Brace had said yes, I don't know what I would have done. For one thing I had to go to the bathroom. For another, I wanted desperately to sneeze, and was holding my finger up against my nose trying to stop it.

Luckily for me, Uncle Brace said, "No, we may need you later. Get your sleep. Mrs. Kingsmark will be out of it for at least five hours." After another few minutes, both pairs of feet left the room by the door near the bed, leaving it open. But they did turn off the light.

I waited what seemed a long time, and resented bitterly having to do so. By the time I crawled out from beneath the bed there would be no chance of Aunt Louisa's being still awake. In fact, she was probably deeply asleep—drugged— even now. But I knew that by speaking the way she did, knowing I was listening, she was sending me the clearest warning she could. And, crouched there, waiting for everyone to be well gone, I sent her my thanks, hoping that in some way, at some time, she would know how grateful I was.

Then I slithered out, trying to make sure that I didn't hit anything or knock anything over. And I didn't. But the moment I removed my finger from underneath my nose, I sneezed. I froze half out from under the bed, waiting to see if anyone had heard. But there was no sound, no steps. So I wriggled the rest of the way, and stood, looking down at Aunt Louisa, who was lying, her face turned away from me, breathing slowly and deeply.

Swiftly I bent and kissed her cheek. "Thanks, Aunt Louisa," I whispered in her ear. She didn't stir, and I didn't expect her to.

Then I ran quietly and quickly across the room, closed the door behind me, releasing the knob slowly, so it wouldn't make a noise, and ran back to my own room. Wolf had been sitting with his nose to the door waiting for me to get back, and I hugged him. "We've got to make plans, Wolf," I whispered. "We've got to get out of here."

As I lay down, the words I'd heard rang over and over again in my mind, *"But it's wicked. She's nothing but a child. . . ."*

I was sure the "Hans-Gunther" Aunt Louisa mentioned was Mr. Gomez, which meant that I was in danger. Aunt Louisa's words came back, *"You're keeping me this way so you can do what you want—what Hans-Gunther wants. . . ."* *"She's nothing but a child. . . ."* And Uncle Brace's cynical *"That's the whole point."*

I had to get in touch with Steve Barrington, and I had to do it immediately. Which meant I would have to ask Carlotta to send my letter. If she refused, perhaps she'd know of some other way to reach Steve. But I didn't have too much time. I had no idea at what time the servants arrived. Or did they live somewhere on the premises? I didn't know that, either. But if I woke early enough I would certainly hear her or some of the other servants coming on their early morning rounds. I had a vague idea that Mr. Hans-Gunther-Gomez had early morning coffee. That decision made, I set the alarm in my clock, lay down, felt the reassurance of Wolf's shoulders near me, and went to sleep.

I woke up before the alarm went off and quickly pushed down the little lever. Then I sat up, and put on my robe. One of the windows in my room faced east, and I looked out over the immense ocean, where the sun, barely risen, made a gold and red track across the shifting surface. Then I walked across to my door, opened it. I looked up and down the hall, and left the door slightly ajar. After that I went back to bed and sat there, waiting for the first sound.

When it came, I couldn't have been more surprised. Because the first sound I heard was that of an envelope sliding across a wooden floor. I had been staring idly through the window, when the slight noise made me turn my head. There, coming under the door, was a white envelope. I was out of bed and across the room in a second, and yanked open the door. Carlotta was there, half straightening. She turned as though to run. But I put my hand out. "Carlotta, please," I whispered. "Please don't go. I have to talk to you. Please come in."

She turned and stared at me.

"Please. I need your help."

For a moment more she stood, looking at me. Then she relaxed. "Very well, miss." She came in. I picked up the envelope and then closed the door. Looking at the front of the envelope I saw my name in slanted handwriting. There was no return address, but I was sure it was from Steve. Tearing open the envelope I read the few words. "Can you meet me at the café in the plaza where we had drinks before at four o'clock this afternoon? Tell Carlotta either way. If you can't make it this afternoon, suggest some other time to Carlotta and she will bring my answer back. Her sister works at our airline ticket office in Sibyl. You can trust her."

"Oh, Carlotta—thank you so much. Tell Steve I'll meet him this afternoon. Can you do that?"

She smiled then. "Yes, miss."

"You won't get into trouble, will you?"

"Not if no one finds out that I am taking messages."

"No one will from me—or Steve."

"I know that."

Impulsively, I put my arms around her and squeezed her. "Thank you. Thank you so much."

After a moment's hesitation, she squeezed me back. "Take care, miss. They're watching you," she whispered.

And then she was gone. I tore the note in tiny pieces and flushed it down the toilet.

Paul and Mr. Gomez were at the breakfast table when I arrived there. Paul looked red-eyed and surly and said nothing when I slipped into my place.

"Good morning, Hilda," Mr. Gomez said. The sea-blue eyes were on me, smiling. Everything I'd heard while crouched under Aunt Louisa's bed came back to me: that I was here because Uncle Brace owed Mr. Gomez money, and that whatever the two of them had in mind involved me.

"Why are you looking at me like that, Hilda?" Mr. Gomez asked quietly.

I jumped a little, realizing I had been staring. It was on the tip of my tongue to give him a truthful answer, but I had a feeling that beneath his puffy lids Paul was watching carefully.

"Sorry, I didn't mean to stare."

Mr. Gomez continued to look at me for a moment, then glanced at Paul and resumed his eating.

"Well, off to the grind," Paul said, getting up.

"What grind?" I asked.

He flushed. "Not everybody is having a vacation."

"I was only teasing."

He muttered, slammed his chair under the table and stalked out. Since I was facing the front, I could see him run down the steps, and then heard the Jeep start up.

"Does he work?" I asked, mostly because I found the silence difficult.

"Not really. He tries. But there isn't a lot he can do. The only manual labor is in the fields, and, considering everything, it's not likely he'd do that. The rest is your uncle's business, and he does that pretty much himself."

"Rachel said he was illegitimate."

"I believe that's true."

"And that his mother was nobody from nowhere."

"As the old world counted things, that was true. She was a girl who started out in his father's office and went into modeling. But I'm surprised to hear you use those terms."

"I'm quoting. And anyway, isn't that your world, too?"

He looked up. "It was. But that's long past. Tell me, what would you like to do today?"

The only thing that mattered today was my four o'clock date with Steve. "Anything," I said. And then, on inspiration, "Why don't we sail this morning and ride this afternoon." If worse came to worst, I could always ride Pronto to the village.

He smiled. "Excellent." He glanced up at the sky. "A little windy for sailing, perhaps, but that should make it interesting."

"Interesting" was a good description of the lively morning that followed. As I watched Mr. Gomez work with the sails and tackle, and tack the boat from side to side, I realized he must have sailed a great deal.

"You've sailed a lot before, haven't you?" I asked.

"Duck!" he called out, and as I hastily obeyed, the boom swung to the other side.

"Come here," he said, pulling me beside him to counterbalance the listing boat. After a moment or so, the balance seemed to be restored. "Yes, I've sailed a lot."

"Where?"

He looked at me, as though weighing what he was going to say. Then, "Germany and Switzerland. We sailed our boats on Lake Geneva quite a lot."

"You're German, aren't you?" I heard my own words with astonishment. How could I be so stupid as to ask this man—who seemed to have his own (unpleasant) motives for being pleasant—a probably unwelcome question.

"Yes," he said after a moment.

"Why do you go under a Spanish name if you're not Spanish?"

"Because we—I—thought it would be more acceptable."

"What do you mean?"

There was a long pause, and then he said, "German names are not always welcome this side of the Atlantic—not after the Second World War . . . and not . . ." he seemed to be choosing his words carefully, "and especially not to those who may have been brought up to believe that all Germans are monsters of evil."

I'd heard my father on this subject, especially when he was talking with Mother, or arguing with some of his friends. He basically believed that monsterdom was part of the genetic equipment of being German—the virus Germanicus, he called it, and I had always more or less agreed with him.

"Well, I'm sorry if it's rude, but aren't they? Look at all the people they tortured and killed in concentration camps."

"Are you including those Germans who were not born until after the war, or were, say, under ten when the war ended?"

We sat, on either side of the tiller and didn't speak for a while. The wind blew, Mr. Gomez watched the sail and the water chopped and slapped around the boat. Far off was the green island. The sky and the water were blue and white. There were no other boats. We were alone.

"How old were you during the war?" I asked.

"I was twenty-three when it started in 1939, twenty-nine when it ended." He paused. "In answer to the question you're probably going to ask next, I was in the Luftwaffe—the German air force."

"Did you bomb places?"

"I was a fighter pilot, so I did not pilot bombers, but I accompanied them."

126

"And you bombed places like England—London and Coventry and other places?"

"Yes." He looked over at me. "Just as your American bombers—and the English RAF, too—bombed Hamburg and Cologne and Dresden."

"But you started the war."

He leaned forward and adjusted the sail. Then when he sat back, "We could argue about that for hours. Historians on both sides have. But tell me, do you feel any the less fond of your own country because you enslaved another race for several hundred years, after dragging them across the world and killing almost half of them in transit?"

"I think it was a terrible thing to do."

"But do you feel any the less part of your country?"

I thought about that a long time. Several of the girls at school were black. One was a particular friend of mine. She once said, "Being an American and being a black is one of those splits you have to learn to live with, but sometimes you feel pretty schizoid about it."

"I have a friend," I said now, "who's black." And I told him what she'd said.

"Yes," he said, "all you can do when your own people do something you know is wrong, is to go on, and hope to create a society where it won't happen again."

"Well, didn't you think what they were doing to the Jews was terrible?"

"I didn't know about the concentration camps. I can't claim to be ignorant of the anti-Semitism, but, along with a lot of others, I didn't particularly question it. And according to books I have read, it was not unknown in your own country. I learned better, after the war. But during the war, I was simply fighting for my country."

"You were fighting for Hitler."

"I was a professional military officer. My family has

been in the military for generations. I was in the air force when war was declared. So of course I fought when the war started. I would have fought no matter who was head of state.''

I didn't say anything, but I wished Father were here with me, so he could answer Mr. Gomez' arguments. "I wish Daddy were here. He could argue with you better," I said finally.

"You don't have to wish for . . . for your father. I'm fully aware of our collective guilt. That might have had something to do with the fact that I left shortly after the war and went to some family property in Brazil. I simply wanted you to understand.''

"Why?" And then, for the first time since we started to talk, I remembered Aunt Louisa's revelations of the night before. "What are you going to try to do with me?" I stood up. The boat wobbled.

"Sit down!" Mr. Gomez thundered, and, reaching up, pulled me back into my seat. "Don't ever do that in a boat. You'll run the danger of sinking it and everyone in it. And these waters have been known to have sharks. . . .'' The last really scared me.

I sat down. For a moment, as I looked at Mr. Gomez, now an old man, I could imagine what he looked like when he was younger: fair-haired, blue-eyed, stern, full of discipline and authority, handsome.

"What did you mean by asking what I was going to do with you?"

I hesitated, and then said, "Last night, I went in to see Aunt Louisa. When Uncle Brace and Williams came in, I got under the bed. And I heard her say that Uncle Brace and you were planning to do something with me, and that Uncle Brace had to because he owes you money.'' I heard my own words with astonishment. I must be really stupid to let him know how much I already knew of his and Uncle Brace's plans. Yet I went on. "And a few nights ago, I was watching through the door when I saw you and Uncle Brace hold Aunt Louisa down, even though she was begging not to have the injection. I think that's *wicked*. And then last night, Uncle Brace told her she was being kept drugged so she couldn't stop you and him doing something with me."

He was steadying the tiller as he said, with an odd one-sided smile, "And yet, hearing all this, you came out alone in a boat with me? Either you didn't believe it, or you are extremely docile, which I find unlikely, or you are definitely stupid, which I know is not true. Which is it?" Then, as I stared at him, he asked, "Would you have gone out on a boat with Brace?"

I knew instantly that I wouldn't. I also knew I wasn't either docile or stupid. Which left the only answer: that deep in me I didn't believe that Mr. Gomez-whoever-he-was would really harm me.

The wind had gone down and the boat had slowed, seeming almost stationary in the choppy water.

"Well," he said, "which is it?"

I didn't answer that. I said, "Were you going to try and take me somewhere?"

"I was going to try and persuade you to visit me for a while at my home in Brazil. It's up in the mountains where coffee is grown, and it's very beautiful. We don't have sailing, but I do have horses and it would, I hope, be a pleasant experience for you."

"Why?" I remembered Aunt Louisa's "She's only a child." "You could be my grandfather."

He smiled again. "With a little stretch I could be your great-grandfather. I'm sixty-seven. But my interest in you is not . . . is something different."

"Well, what is it?" And then from nowhere, I asked, "What color was your hair?"

He smiled. "Fair, like yours." He paused and his smile faded. "You are not, as you think, David and Susan Tashoff's natural daughter. They adopted you. We have met before, you know, during the first four years of your life. Sometimes I think you almost remember it." He paused for a moment, as though trying to find words. I knew what they were before he found them, just as I finally understood the odd feeling I sometimes had when I looked at him, and the sense of an old memory stirring.

"You see," he said, finally finding the words, "I am your real father. You are my daughter."

9

"No!" I cried, even though I knew it was true. I wanted so much for it not to be true. I couldn't bear the thought of my father, the man I had always thought of as my father, not being my real father. "It's not true!"

"You know it is. All you have to do is look in the mirror."

I twisted away from him and stared out at the ocean. My old dislike of boats turned out to be more prophetic than I had dreamed. There was no way I could do what I was longing to do—run—run away from this man and his voice and the things he was saying.

"Is it so terrible?" he asked.

"Yes." I didn't even turn around. "You don't understand. Daddy—my *real* father, I mean the one I always thought was my real father—we've always been so close."

"Nothing I have told you changes that."

"Yes it does. It does. For one thing—" The words popped out of nowhere, "It means that my sister Juliet has a . . . relationship with him I don't."

"That's a little petty, isn't it?"

I never even dreamed that I was jealous of Juliet that way. But there'd been so many family jokes about how close

131

Daddy and I were, just as Juliet and Mother were. . . . Mother. I hadn't even thought of her. And yet, he had said I was not the daughter of either. I thought of Mother with her understanding, her dry sense of humor, her kindness, her brown eyes and curly brown hair, like Juliet's. And then I thought of Juliet, who was really no longer my little sister, who belonged to them much more than I did. . . . And the tears started rolling down my cheeks.

"Is it that bad?"

I turned and looked at him. "Yes. It's awful to think that you've been one person all your life and then find out you haven't been that person."

"You are exactly the same as you've always been. I'm sorry this was such a bad shock." He hesitated, then put out his hand, "Hilda—"

But I shrank away from it, hating him for what he'd just taken away. "Don't!" I saw in his eyes how much I'd hurt him, but I didn't care, in fact I was glad. "I want to go back. Now. And then I want to go home. And I will *not* come with you to Brazil."

"All right." His face looked strained, but his voice was almost indifferent. He moved the tiller, adjusted the jib sheet, and turned the boat. The wind had not died as much as I had thought, and we went back at a spanking pace.

When we were about halfway to the shore he said, "Do you have any questions you'd like me to answer?"

"No."

"Well, in the future, when you have your own children, you might come to regret that answer, so I shall tell you a few things about who you are, at least as far as your biological parents are concerned." He paused. I knew he was hoping I would acknowledge in some way what he was telling me, but I was filled with anger at him, so I continued to stare ahead.

"My real name is Hans-Gunther von Rucker. We are an old Prussian family, but since both I and my father were only children you are the last of the line. Your mother was an American, and Jewish. Her name was Rebecca Stern. She was an old girlfriend of your father's in their college days. She went into the Peace Corps and came to South America. By the time I knew her, eighteen years ago, she had left the Peace Corps and was working with some of the Catholic Relief Agencies. Fortunately, none of the people on my property were in need of her services, but she was quite political in her approach, and I represented everything—on two continents—that she disliked and disapproved of. Nevertheless we fell in love and had an affair. You were the result of that. I wanted us to marry—I was a widower and had no ties, and wanted her to get a divorce from the husband she had already left when I met her. I think she was going to, when she had the accident . . . from which she finally died. Before she died she wrote to your parents, asking if they would adopt you. But she let them believe that you were the daughter of her former husband. I knew nothing of this. She lived in São Paulo and I lived up in the mountains. But I used to visit you both all the time, although none of her friends knew about our relationship. When she died, she left instructions that you were to be placed in a convent until your parents could come and collect you. You were then about three and a half. I went to the convent to see you, and to try and persuade the nuns to let you come and live with me. But the nuns were adamant. You were registered as the daughter of your mother's husband, who also lived in São Paulo. He certainly didn't want to take you, and I had no proof that I had any right to. Also, I had had a heart attack, and I was finally convinced by the Mother Superior of the convent that for me, a widower of fifty-four, with a heart attack behind me, to take you and bring you up, would be grossly unfair to you. So I gave in. But there is something I want you to know. . . ."

He waited a moment and then went on, "The last time I saw you before you came here was in that convent. You had on a blue dress I had given you. You may find this hard to believe, but you were quite devoted to me. You thought I had come to take you home, and you cried bitterly when I told you I couldn't, but that other people would be coming soon who would give you a new home. It was the hardest thing I have ever done. And when I left, you ran after me, crying . . . do you have no memory of that?"

And the scene that had moved at the back of my memory tunnel shifted again and I saw myself running and crying after a tall figure, filled with desolation and anger . . . my nightmare.

"Do you?"

I didn't want to say anything, to acknowledge him in any way, but I said, "You left me. I do remember. You went off and left me. And I hated you."

"Yes. I'm sure you did, *Liebchen*."

The German word jarred loose something else. I saw myself again, this time in shorts and a pink T-shirt. A tall fair man was leaning over me. . . . *"Liebchen . . ."* he said, and kissed me.

I was really crying now, and all I wanted to do was to get away. To my relief, the boat glided up to the pier. Before he could move, I was up on the pier and running, running, running away from the man that in my now clearer memory I had run after so desperately long ago.

But, two hours later, lying on the ground not far from the stables, but hidden by trees, I knew there were questions I still had to ask, questions about the man I had always thought of as my father. "He must know," I said aloud, and sat up. My being here, his strange behavior, everything, would make sense if he had just found out who my . . . my biological father really was. And where did Aunt Louisa and that awful Uncle Brace come into it? According to what I had overheard, they cooperated because von Rucker—I had now to call him by his real name—because von Rucker had blackmailed them, using their indebtedness to him as a weapon. I wanted to believe that, but wasn't quite able to. Like the woman who von Rucker said was my mother, I had been brought up by my adoptive father, to hate everything my biological father represented. Added to that was my own memory of his abandoning me. Yet with all that I couldn't quite see him as a blackmailer.

Finally I got to my feet and went towards the house. Wolf, who had been outside investigating various smells, met me. "You can come riding with me this afternoon," I started. And then wondered if it was safe for him.

"Never mind," I said, looking down at him. "We'll have lots of exercise in the States." At that I remembered that Mr. Go—that von Rucker had enabled me to have Wolf. It was all so muddling, and nobody, including me, seemed to be a clear-cut good guy. Absurdly, and suddenly, I remembered a favorite rhyme of my mother's . . . my adoptive mother's:

> There is so much good in the worst of us,
> And so much bad in the best of us,
> That it hardly behooves any of us
> To talk about the rest of us.

It was the kind of thing Mother believed in, and practiced. Not Father—to him there were the good guys and the bad guys, and the latter deserved all the badmouthing they got.

The funny thing was, in this, as in so much else, I had completely identified with him.

As I reached the house I hesitated and glanced at my watch. Two-fifteen. Lunch would be over now, but the two men would almost surely be there still and I intended to ask them questions.

Von Rucker had said that my mother had let my parents believe that my biological father was her former husband. Did they know now he wasn't? That letter with the South American stamp hung in my mind. And in my memory, once again, I saw my father's face go still and white. Certainty filled me now as much as though I had read the letter. But who sent it? And why now?

Still I hesitated, waiting at the foot of the steps, with Wolf beside me. I was to meet Steve at four o'clock, and nothing must interfere with that. Two forces tugged at me. On one side were the answers I wanted, powerful imperatives to go in and force them from von Rucker and Brace Kingsmark. But pulling against that was my meeting with Steve, less than an hour and a half away. Once I was inside the house, was I absolutely certain I would be able to keep that date? Brace Kingsmark was lord of the island and unpredictable. Seeing Steve meant my own freedom to get away. The answers would have to wait for a moment. . . .

I looked down at Wolf. "I'm afraid of taking you, Wolfie." And remembered again the dart that was, I hoped, still in my saddlebag. I didn't want to leave him, either. Why I felt this so strongly I didn't know. But I found myself unwilling to leave Wolf behind in a house that I was doing my best to escape from. "All right, Wolfie. But we're going down the highway, and I want you to stick close." Wolf wagged his tail.

Leaving the house, I ran over to the stables and began saddling Pronto. As I took the saddle off its stand, I ran my hand down into the saddlebag to find out if the dart were still there. It was, I pulled it out, and I was holding it in my hand, looking at it, about to touch the tip of my finger to the point, when there was a shout behind me, "Do not touch! Do not touch!"

I turned. Pierre, the groom, was running towards me.

"Do not touch," he cried again. Then he came up to me and snatched the arrow out of my hand. "See," he indicated the end where there was the yellowish stain. "That is poison. It pricks you, you get very sick, maybe you die."

"Somebody shot that at me when I was out riding before. You know, the day I came back late and everyone was here—all the people from Sibyl."

"Why you not say?"

"I didn't know it was poisonous. I just thought—I guess I was so angry at something else, that I forgot about it. But Pierre, somebody, a little boy from a cabin in the woods, offered Pronto here some sugar with the same yellowish stuff on it. Who wants to kill us? Why?"

"I know nothing. I dunno anything. You stay out of woods. Not safe for people at big house. Not safe."

"I know my uncle is, well, a tyrannical monster." I thought about what I'd just said to somebody who worked for him. But it was true. "He is. I know that. Is that why somebody shot that at me? To get back at him?"

"I know nothing. Nothing at all." And Pierre, who was backing, was out the door.

With the words, "You stay out of woods. Not safe for people at big house," ringing in my ears, I finished saddling Pronto, but knew that I was not going to take Wolf. They already hated the dogs from Tradewinds.

"No, Wolf. You're going to stay. I'm not taking you." The surest way to keep him safe would be to take him up to the house and lock him in my room. But I did not want to go into the house until I had seen Steve, and Wolf had been out-side on the grounds before without incurring danger, so I had no fear for him in the immediate vicinity. However, I had to keep him from following us, so after I had led Pronto out, and tied him to a post, I pushed Wolf back into the stable and closed all the doors. "I'm sorry, darling," I said, as his yelps rose. "But I want you alive." Someone, I knew, would sooner or later come along, but by that time Pronto and I would be out of sight and Wolf could just wait for our return.

This time I took Pronto through the woods and out onto the highway as quickly as possible. I knew I shouldn't ride Pronto on the asphalt, but I remembered the bridle path run-ning parallel to the road, and I rode Pronto down the length of the island on that. Twice I was scared by hearing a car coming behind us, and plunged Pronto through the bushes and back among the trees, something he did not enjoy. But I couldn't be sure the car didn't contain Uncle Brace or that awful Schmidt, or even von Rucker come to find me and force me back.

Finally, alternately trotting and cantering, I arrived in the village. I glanced at my watch; it was four o'clock. Ideally, there should be a stable where I could rest Pronto until I had seen Steve. Slowly I trotted towards the town square. The streets were fairly full of people walking and standing, chat-ting in groups. They looked cheerful. But the moment they saw Pronto and me everyone stopped and stared. And there grew a silence. Rarely had I felt so uncomfortable. Well, I thought, silence or no, I was going to walk Pronto and cool him down, and then find out if there was a stable. Or better still, wait until I saw Steve. He would know, and people would probably be a lot more forthcoming to him than they were with me.

So I slid off Pronto's back, and, holding his reins, started walking him slowly around the square. There were no other horses, but there were one or two mules tied up outside various stores, which I found vaguely comforting. At least large animals ridden by humans were not unknown. But, although the talking started again it seemed lower and did not have the casual liveliness I had noticed before they'd seen me. But I ignored everyone, staring more or less straight ahead, and hoped that I would not come face to face with anyone from Tradewinds.

Suddenly, as Pronto and I turned a corner, I saw Steve. He was getting out of his car, which he had parked not far from the cathedral.

"Steve!" I called.

He looked up, grinned, and then waved. After locking his car he came over to us. "That's a very patrician mode of travel you have there." As he talked he stroked Pronto on his face and neck. "Wait till we get to the café, I'll give you some sugar," he said.

"Steve, do you know that somebody tried to poison him?"

He stared at me, his hand still on Pronto's neck. "When? Why?"

"It was when I saw the woman and the little boy and somebody shot a dart at me, which was also poisoned." I realized, as I blurted all this out, it must sound absolutely wild, the ravings of an imagination that had lost all touch with reality. "I know it sounds crazy," I said weakly, "but it's true."

He drew his hand along Pronto's nose once more. "It does sound wild, but not if you know that house up there." He hesitated and smiled. "And not if you know you. Which I do. I'm glad to say." Some red stole up into his cheek.

"So'm I—glad to say, that I know you," I finished, and then we both laughed.

"Come on. Let's have our drink. We can put Pronto into José's barn. It won't be what he's used to, but the hay and the water are just as good."

"I knew you'd know where to put him. Everybody in the square stopped talking when Pronto and I rode in."

"People showing up on highly bred horses aren't usual in their daily lives. Only the people at Tradewinds and their guests do that. And of course, even if you walked in without Pronto, they'd stop, because you're from the big house. You must have noticed that."

"Yes," I said. "I have. I'll tell you about it. Where's José's barn?"

"Just down this street a little. The village is really only the square. Right outside it's farmland. What's the matter?" Because I had stopped.

"Steve, you don't think that anyone would hurt Pronto, do you? Knowing that he belonged to the Kingsmarks. I mean, like I told you, somebody already tried to poison him."

We'd both stopped. Steve looked over Pronto absent-mindedly while he was, very obviously, thinking. I, too, was thinking—about what a nice build Steve had, and how attractively his dark hair curled—not too much, just right.

Finally Steve said, "No, I don't think anyone will hurt Pronto."

"You don't seem awfully sure."

"I'm sure that nobody will hurt Pronto as long as he is in José's charge. What I had to think about, is whether José himself would be singled out for unpleasantness by your charming uncle and his guest for having given him shelter."

When he said, "and his guest" I knew he meant von Rucker, and my heart gave a funny "thunk." I had an awful lot to tell Steve.

"Oh," I said. "I see."

140

"But I don't think he'll suffer. After all, he can always say that you, a member of their family, insisted on his keeping the horse for an hour or so." Steve grinned. "And they could hardly expect a mere peon to stand up against that."

10

José's house and barn were, indeed, only a few hundred yards north of the square—the side farthest away from Tradewinds. Also, José turned out to be a tall, muscular young man, with the same bandit's mustache that Steve had once had, and fluent English. Pronto was led into a comfortable-looking stall, his saddle and bridle were taken off, and he was given some water and a wisp or so of hay to keep him happy.

"José, this is Hilda Tashoff," Steve said, when we had left the barn. "She's a niece of Brace Kingsmark. If anybody wants to know why one of the The House's horses is here in your barn, tell them it was her wish to put him here while she was busy in the village." I had noticed before that Tradewinds was always "The House" to people on the island.

"I will be happy to do so." It struck me that José was very far from being what I had always thought of as a peon. Not knowing quite how to put this thought, I said, "Your English is wonderful."

"It should be," Steve said. "He teaches at the school here, and will one day teach at the university in Sibyl."

"Oh." I discovered that José was looking at me with a

slightly ironic glint in his eye. "I'm sorry," I said. "I didn't know."

"We are not all brainless peasants, Miss Tashoff."

"I didn't think you were," I said indignantly.

"She's not like her uncle and aunt and that Nazi up there," Steve said cheerfully. "She's like us."

José bowed slightly. "My apologies."

As Steve and I walked away I said, "You meant Schmidt, didn't you, when you said 'that Nazi up there'?"

"Actually, I meant that Hans-Gunther von something or other, passing himself off as Gomez. But there's Schmidt, too, of course."

We continued in silence for a while until we hit the square and turned towards the café.

"You're awfully quiet," Steve said. He stopped and reached out his arm, stopping me. "Did I say something that bothered you?"

"It's just that I have an awful lot to tell you."

"All right." He glanced up. "Let's get ourselves a table and order something, and then you can tell me."

"Now," he said, when we each had a soda in front of us. "Tell me."

I had meant to begin at the beginning and work slowly up. But my mouth opened and I heard myself say, "Oh Steve, that man, von Rucker, the one you called a Nazi, he's my father. I didn't believe him at first when he said that this morning, but I've been thinking and thinking ever since, and I have a terrible feeling it's true." I was trying very hard not to cry, but I didn't quite succeed. I groped in my jeans pocket for a handkerchief, but there didn't seem to be one there.

"Here," Steve said, handing me a thin white linen square with blue pinstripes. I accepted it gratefully, and wiped off my tears, and when I could speak said, "Thanks." I looked at it. "It seems too pretty to spoil." And started flowing again.

"Now listen," Steve said, when I had things under control. "Begin at the beginning. That's quite . . . quite a revelation you made. Did you know this before?"

I shook my head. "He said that was the reason that my Aunt Louisa—who really is my mother's cousin—invited me here. I think they owe huge sums of money to von Rucker, and he wanted to see me. He said," I took a deep breath, "he said that my mother—my real mother—was in the Peace Corps in South America, and disapproved of him because he was a German and had been in the German air force and all that, but they had an affair and I was the result. And she lived in São Paulo, working with the relief agencies, and he used to come and see us. Anyway, she died after an accident when I was about three and a half, and he wanted to adopt me, but she had written to my father—to my adoptive father and mother—and asked them to adopt me. She'd been an old girlfriend of my father's. But she let them believe that I was the child of her former husband because she knew that my father would have a fit if he'd known that I was the daughter of a former German air force officer. My father's Jewish, and thinks all Germans are Nazis. . . ."

"Ye gods!" Steve said, and rubbed his hair. "What a story!" He looked at me. "And you believe him, now?"

I nodded, blowing my nose on his handkerchief.

"Why?"

"Because—well, I'd better begin at the beginning—before the beginning." And I told him about the letter that had come and how Daddy had reacted and how he'd been different ever since. "And there's something else, too. I look like him—von Rucker I mean. Also, I didn't exactly remember him, but I had a funny feeling when I looked at him, like there was something I could *almost* remember.

Like something far back in my mind. He told me that the last time he saw me, which was in a convent in São Paulo, where I'd been taken after my mother, my biological mother, had died, he told me then that I would have a new family. But that I had been quite devoted to him, and that when he left, I ran after him, crying. And Steve, when he said that, I knew it was true. I didn't remember all of it, but I remember the awful feeling, of somebody I loved terribly leaving me, abandoning me. . . ." I blew my nose again.

There was a silence, then Steve said, "Funny—do you remember when we were sitting here last time I asked you if you were related to him. And I think I asked that because something about you reminded me of him."

"Did you meet him?"

"Yes. He stopped at Sibyl Airport to refuel. His plane is registered under the name of von something or other, but I heard via the island telegraph that he was calling himself Gomez, and I assumed it was because he didn't want to be kidnapped by Israeli agents or some such. Which is probably unfair to him, but the name von, put together with that rather Prussian manner and the fact that he came from South America made me think of Eichmann and Barbie and a few others."

"He says he didn't know about the camps until after the war, and that he fought because he was a professional officer, and would have no matter who was head of the country."

"You don't hate him, do you?"

I shook my head. "No." And then I burst out, "I don't know *what* I feel about him. It's all muddled."

Steve put out his hand and closed it over mine, which was on the table. "Look, be easy on yourself. This is one helluva shock for you. I can understand why you don't know how you feel about anybody—'' he grinned ''—present company excluded, of course.''

I looked into Steve's eyes and noticed for the first time that they were a greenish blue and slightly tilted up at the corners. I'd never been very good about noticing the details of people's faces, but I could have drawn his.

''Hi,'' he said, and laughed, and closed his hand around mine.

''Hi!'' I said, and could feel the blood coming up my neck to my cheeks.

It was the whistle that brought me around. I jumped and looked to one side. A bunch of islanders were standing watching us, broad grins on their faces. I snatched my hand back.

Steve grinned. ''It's not possible to be private on this island. You could go into six rooms within rooms with no windows and close every door and still the island would know by the next morning what you'd said and done and with whom.''

''That's pretty awful. Like living in a goldfish bowl.''

''Lots of people live like that. Sibyl, which is much larger, is like that. I guess it's because you come from New York that you find it alarming.'' He hesitated. ''Can we go back a bit? There are a couple of things I'd like to ask.''

''Sure.''

''If von Rucker was that fond of you, when you were a baby, why didn't he keep you?''

''Because, he said, he was fairly old—fifty-three or something like that—and had already had one heart attack. He said the nuns at the convent persuaded him that it would be fairer to let me go. He said it was the hardest thing he ever did.'' Somehow it seemed important to add that.

''You believe him?''

I looked up into the blue-green eyes that were watching me. They were penetrating, but kind.

"Yes. I do. I wish like anything the whole thing weren't true. That I really was the daughter of my parents. But it has to be true, because I can't think why they'd let me come to such a place unless it were."

"What did you think at the time—when you left for here and they left for somewhere else? I mean, is that usual? Do they often go one place and you another?"

"Well, Daddy's always rushing off to arrange for a book, or do research or something—he's an editor with a publishing house, I thought he'd gone to investigate indigenous guerrilla movements or some such, and I know Mummy always likes to go with him. And when the letter—the letter inviting me here—arrived, she made it sound like I was going to some hotsy-totsy vacation place, like maybe Bermuda or a warm Bar Harbor. . . ."

"But did you *want* to come?"

"No. Not really. But summer had come, I'd had flu, Mother wanted to go to South America with Father, my sister Juliet was going to camp, and my parents certainly wouldn't let me stay in New York alone. So, I said I'd come."

"I gather they sort of twisted your arm."

"Not really. I kept thinking how enthusiastic I *ought* to be. It *sounded* fine."

"Was it that letter that changed your father towards you?"

"No. The first letter did that."

"Before the arrangements were made for you to come here."

"Yes."

"So the first letter had something to do with your coming here, too." He made it as a statement, not a question.

I hadn't quite put the two letters together like that until this moment. I had been sure Father had changed towards me as a result of the first letter, and that I had been invited here because of the second. And yet . . . I realized now that part of my anger against my parents for sending me here was the fear that they did so because my father's attitude towards me—his love for me—had changed. Before that letter that altered everything, they wouldn't have dreamed of sending me by myself to a place like this. . . . The first person who would have refused even to consider it was my father. . . . I could almost hear him, *"What do you mean you're willing to send Hilda to some Caribbean dump with a remote cousin you haven't seen for years and her unknown husband? How do we know how they'll treat Hilda. . . ?"* With him, I had always been special—until a few weeks ago. Then, whatever that letter said, it must have made it all right for him to let me come here. . . . Once more trying to talk suddenly became difficult.

"Hey. I'm sorry," Steve said. "I didn't mean to upset you again."

I wiped my cheeks and blew my nose. "I'm sure that letter, the first one, told Daddy—my father—that I was the daughter of some German officer, and that that made him different to me. He didn't care then what happened, and Mother went along."

Steve stared at me for a moment. "Let's give them the benefit of the doubt. Maybe your aunt really did describe this place like a super vacation spot. I mean, can't you imagine? *We have this charming country house, with swimming pool and stables, and young people around, etcetera, etcetera. . . ."*

"What young people? The ones from Sibyl?"

"And Paul Kingsmark. Is he still as charming as ever, by the way?"

"He's been drinking an awful lot. Rachel, one of the girls from Sibyl, said that he was the illegitimate son of Uncle Brace's brother, and that his mother was a nobody from nowhere, and that he's trying to be snobbier than anyone else to . . . to sort of overcompensate."

"Well . . ." Steve rubbed his nose. "I guess that could be true. The slightly lower class person who gets into an exclusive club, wants all the rules stiffened to make sure nobody else of his own kind can make it."

I giggled a little. "That's awful. But I think it's probably true. I've been feeling a little sorry for him, because he's gotten drunk a few times and made a fool of himself and been put down by Uncle Brace in front of me and Mr. G—von Rucker."

"Don't feel too sorry. I don't mean to sound vengeful, but I have a feeling that if he can make up lost points by beating up on you in some way, he will. About your parents . . ."

A terrible feeling of abandonment swept over me, and for a moment I felt sick.

"Hilda?" Steve leaned over again and this time put his hand around mine in my lap. "Don't look like that. It's probably not the way you think it is."

But I was being gripped by a queer feeling—as though all this had happened before, and was part of a script that had been written. . . .

"Hilda!" Steve said again.

"Have you ever felt that something was *fated* to happen and that you couldn't do anything about it?" I said.

"No. And furthermore, I don't believe it. Hilda, you always have a choice. Always. What is it you're thinking about, anyway? What is it you're afraid of?"

But the nightmarish vision had gone as suddenly as it came, and the odd part was, I couldn't recall it. "You're going to think I'm crazy, but it was something that . . . that came over me for a moment, but it's gone now.'' I said slowly, ''It had something to do with the two fathers, my own, I mean, my adoptive, and von Rucker. . . .''

''There's something else I wanted to ask you. You mentioned that somebody aimed a dart at you. When was that?''

''The day the young people all came from Sibyl. I got isolated from the others and then lost and when I was riding along one of the narrow bridle paths, an arrow came whizzing past me and stuck in a tree nearby. I took it out and saw that it had a stone point which was smeared in something sort of yellowish-beige. Then, when I came to the cabin in the woods, one of the kids there, a little boy, ran up and offered Pronto a cube of sugar, but before Pronto could touch it, a woman came and snatched it back and yanked the little boy away. But before she did, I saw that the sugar cube was smeared with the same guck that had been on the arrow.''

''Do you have the arrow?''

''Yes, but it's in Pronto's saddlebag. And when I got it out this morning, and was looking at the point, about to touch it with my finger, the groom yelled at me not to touch it. And kept saying that nobody from the Big House was safe in the woods.''

''If it's what I think it is, it's a local poison that may not kill you, but will certainly make you awfully sick, in fact you'd lose control of your muscles for a while.''

''But why attack me with it, and poor Pronto?''

''Because you are a member of The House, and as such, are the enemy. You know your Uncle Brace is not exactly the island's great benefactor. He's turned I don't know how many people out of houses they—or their families—have lived in for generations, just because he wanted to build horse trails or make a swimming pool, or grow tobacco in the few feet they and their families had occupied. It's not unlike what the English did to the Irish so that they could use the people's land for grazing their horses, or what the Scotch did during a discreditable episode of Scottish history called 'The Clearances,' when the landlords removed their tenants from the land, put them, literally and physically, on the shores of Scotland—hundreds and hundreds of them—to be picked up by ships that then took them to the colonies."

"That's really ghastly. Why are people so awful?"

"Power corrupts, etcetera." He smiled a little. "You've heard that."

"Yes." I was suddenly remembering what Rachel had said: *"I think you ought to figure out what it is that your Uncle Brace wants so badly that requires you to be here."* Now I said to Steve, "Rachel said something sort of like that," and I told him what it was.

"And do you think you know what it is?"

"I suppose, to have Mr. G—von Rucker wipe out his debt."

"Umm. I wonder. I suppose if the debt is big enough it could certainly be a reason." He looked at me for a moment. "What would you like me to do? How can I help?"

I stared at him because although I was hoping he would ask exactly that, now that he had, I didn't know how to answer.

He put out his hand again and clasped mine. "Hilda, if you had your choice now as to what you'd like most to do, what would you say?"

As I continued not to answer, he asked gently, "Talk to your parents? Your real parents?"

"Yes," I burst out. It didn't matter that I was angry with them, with my father particularly. Nothing mattered now except to talk to them, to make sure that my world was still there.

151

"Okay. Let's go." And Steve got up, putting some money on the café table.

I got up, too. "Where are we going? To somebody's house?"

"No. Nobody's phone is safe. Your charming uncle has spies everywhere, including the island switchboard. No, we're going to Sibyl."

A great rush of joy and freedom filled me. "Terrific!" And then I remembered Pronto . . . and Wolf, and stopped. "But what about Pronto?"

"Don't worry about him. If necessary, José will see that he comes to no harm and gets back."

"Won't Uncle Brace take it out on him in some way?"

"José is one of the few people on the island who isn't dependent on him. The schoolteacher's salary is paid in Sibyl. And José could get a job teaching at the college any time he wanted. He only keeps on at this because he thinks the children of the island need to have a few facts brought to their attention. To say nothing of schooling. Your uncle would probably let them go without any education as long as he could."

"But Wolf," I said. "They'll kill him. If I don't go back, either Schmidt will get him or the islanders will."

"Who said anything about your not going back? All I'm going to do is fly you to Sibyl so you can have a quiet hour or two at a phone safe from your uncle. You can find out where your parents are and then call them. I'll lend you the money if you don't have it. Anyway, it'll go on the airline account."

"You're wonderful!" I said. We had got to the car, and without thinking I flung my arms around him and hugged him. Then, embarrassed, I started to withdraw but couldn't, because Steve was hugging me back. Then he kissed me and held me for a moment.

There was a burst of applause.

"Oh!" I said, and stepped back.

He grinned and opened his car door. "I told you there's no such thing as privacy. Now get in and let's get going."

It was a short ride to the airport, and I rode there in a general state of bliss.

"The plane's ready to go, I saw to that before I came into the town," Steve said, as he got out of the car. "It's right over there." And he indicated an even smaller plane than the one I'd flown in with him.

We walked over to the plane that was sitting at the end of the small runway. My cloud of bliss was still there but reality in the form of anxiety over my parents and Wolf was beginning to bump it a little.

"Okay," Steve said. "In you get!"

I climbed in and then Steve followed. He turned on the engine and the propeller blades, but that was as far as we got, because just as the plane started to move, a car came through the trees lining the runway straight across the plane's path and parked in front of it. Then the door opened and Uncle Brace got out.

11

"Well," Steve said, braking just in time. "I guess—for the moment—that takes care of that."

"What are we going to do?" I asked, watching Uncle Brace come up to the plane. Paul, I noticed, was driving the car Uncle Brace had come in.

Steve glanced at me. "See what develops, I guess. I'm sorry about this." Suddenly he looked younger, almost my own age.

Uncle Brace yanked open the plane door just behind our seats. "Get out, Hilda!"

I don't like being ordered around. I looked back at him. "Why should I? Steve's a friend of mine. If he offers to take me for a plane ride, why shouldn't I enjoy it?"

"Because your father—your real father, Baron von Rucker—thanks to you has had a heart attack—his second. We've sent for the doctor and he may or may not be able to survive this. The important thing is, he wants to see you. And I'm going to see that he gets his wish."

"I'm sorry about the heart attack." I paused, realizing that I really was sorry. "But you still don't have the right to order me around."

"On this island my wishes are observed. And you are my guest."

"Not because I wanted to be. I didn't want to come, and as I told you, I want to go home."

"You will go home when I am ready for you to go home. Now get out of the plane."

I don't know what made me do it, but I turned towards the other seat. "Steve?"

He just looked at me. "Sorry," he said finally, "I can't help you." He leaned back of me and slid the short deplaning ladder in place. Mr. Helpful, I thought, feeling sick. Slowly I got up, went back of my seat, and then down the steps out of the plane. Uncle Brace's hand gripped my arm as I stepped onto the ground. Then he looked back at Steve.

"I will be in touch with your uncle about your share in this."

"My uncle is not responsible for my actions," Steve said. "This was my idea, not his."

"But it *is* his plane."

"It's not his fault if I stole it."

Having been in bliss less than half an hour before, I stood there, miserable and ashamed as I listened to Steve's conciliatory tone. My hero, I thought. And then, just like my hero father, sending me into this mess because of something I couldn't help, and my other hero father, von Rucker, leaving me in the convent . . . And the scene that had hovered far back in my memory sprang forward. Much clearer now, I saw myself as the child I had been, dropping the doll or toy bear I had been holding, reaching out to the tall man who was walking away from me faster than I could run after him. . . . But stronger than the image was the feeling, the feeling of being left, abandoned, deserted . . . the feeling I had now.

Uncle Brace pushed me in the front of the car beside Paul,

and then got in the back himself. "Lock the doors," he said to Paul. Paul reached to the side door and flicked a lever that controlled the electronic switches. "And put on the air conditioner," my uncle added. Because in the car, with the windows closed, the moist air was stifling.

The car moved away from the runway and went back towards the trees. As we left, I heard the plane engines start. I turned, and saw the plane move forward, then pick up speed. Just as we drove out of sight I saw the plane rise and the wheels start to lift and fold in. So Steve was gone. He was free. He was free to leave me and he left. . . . A voice in my mind told me that there was nothing else he could do. There was no way he could jump his plane over Uncle Brace's car. But I remembered again the conciliatory tone of his voice. When the pinch came, he was a good boy and kept himself out of trouble. . . . Not fair, not fair, my inner voice said, but I didn't listen.

"So," Uncle Brace said, as though reading my mind, "your boyfriend didn't stick up for you, did he?"

"What could he do?" I asked indignantly, swinging to the other side.

"Oh, there were one or two things, weren't there, Paul?" And he leaned forward and gave Paul an affectionate slap on the back. I glanced at Paul's face. He had a weak smile on his face.

"Like what?" I asked.

"Like running the plane into the car," Uncle Brace said. "If he'd really wanted to get you out he could have done that."

"And what would he have got me out with, if his plane was wrecked in the process?" I was looking at Uncle Brace in the rearview mirror.

"The car would have been hurt a lot worse than the plane, and the plane might still have been able to fly. And if the plane was smashed, there are other planes in various hangars in the field. He could have flown you out in one of those. That's what I'd have done if I wanted to get my girl out of there.''

"Well, Paul," I said, looking sideways at him. "Would you have been a hero?''

"Sure,'' he replied, changing gears as we started up the long slow incline to Tradewinds. "He could have done something. Uncle Brace is right. He knuckled under pretty easily.''

Since that simply confirmed what I thought anyway, I gave up and didn't say anything. We rode the rest of the way in silence.

"Now,'' Uncle Brace said to me, as we stood in the front hall. "Your father is in that room in there. We converted it into a bedroom so he didn't have to go upstairs. You will go in and tell him that you are looking forward to going to Brazil with him. If he believes that, that the two of you will be in Brazil together, he may . . . his chances of recovery are better.'' Uncle Brace gripped my arm again, the fingers closing on my flesh. I tried to pull away, but the harder I pulled, the more his fingers pinched. "He must recover. Do you understand that? He *must!*''

"Why?'' I said. And then, "You're hurting me!''

"Because my plans require it.''

I gave my arm a sharp pull, but the cruel fingers bit in even harder. "If you do not do as I say, I will have Wolf killed, and will take you to watch it. Do you hear me?''

"You're insane,'' I said.

"Perhaps. Others have said that. I don't care. What I care about is having my way. You will do as I told you, or—Wolf dies. Do you understand?''

It was as though I had a prevision of that horrible deed. "Yes,'' I said.

"Your father must recover. That's all you have to remember. If he gets well enough to be flown to Brazil, with you and your dog, then everything will be all right. If not, your dog will die, and you will not get off this island. Do you understand?"

"Yes." Believing now that he was insane, in a curious way, helped. I no longer had to find any kind of logic in what he was doing. I simply had to accept that he was a maniac and go on from there. But while that aspect of the pressure was removed, my realization of my own danger increased. I began to realize that if Uncle Brace were, as I had come to believe, truly mad, then my chances of escape were considerably less.

"Now," he said. "You will go into his bedroom after me. You will assure him of how much you want to go with him to Brazil, and how your happiness depends on his getting well. And you will make him believe it."

"Yes," I said.

"Good. Raoul, you will stay with Miss von Rucker, now, until I send for her."

"Yes, sir."

I looked at the darkish man with a gun in his belt and his uniform khaki shirt and pants. He looked like a hired thug, and probably would behave like one, I thought, and wondered where he'd been in the past days since I had come to the island. I certainly hadn't seen him before.

As though he had read my mind, Uncle Brace said, "Raoul does not come from the island and has no ties here. He would therefore not be reluctant to—er—prevent anyone of the island from reaching you, or you reaching them, if I make myself clear."

"Quite clear." I eyed Raoul, hoping that he would be young enough for me to try and make an ally of him. But while he was young, there was something in his face and eyes that made me shiver.

"And don't try anything with Raoul," Uncle Brace said. "He doesn't understand English and he has instructions to stop you if you try." Then he said something rapidly in a language that sounded Spanish but was not, and which I took to be Portuguese.

"All right. I'll be back in a moment."

I sat on a chair staring at my lap while Uncle Brace was inside the next room. I could hear voices, but I could not hear what was said. Raoul had moved nearer to me and was standing, his legs apart, only a few yards from me. When I raised my eyes I got either a stare back that made my blood run cold, or an ugly, mocking smile. Raoul, I felt, would love to stop me from doing something. So I kept my head down. There was no one else around, and no other sound in the house. With a pang, I wondered where Wolf was and whether he was still alive. Then I decided he must be. He was the weapon Uncle Brace had over me, and so long as he had that weapon—and no longer—Wolf would be all right. I thought about Aunt Louisa, almost certainly lying drugged in her room upstairs, and Paul, with his oddly white face, agreeing with everything Uncle Brace had said. And Williams. Either she liked her grim work, or she was too terrorized to appear not to. But what about Carlotta? Had Uncle Brace discovered that she had brought me the message from Steve? I pulled my mind away. The thought of Steve was like an intensely sore spot. I had believed he was strong and on my side, and he had caved in like a piece of paper.

The door opened. "Hilda?" Uncle Brace said abruptly. "Your father wants to see you." I went into the room ahead of him and heard him close the door behind us.

Von Rucker was lying in a wide bed, half propped up on many pillows. He looked white and drawn and much, much older than before. When the door closed he opened his eyes and saw me.

"Hilda," he said.

Uncle Brace went over to the side of the bed. "Hilda has come to see you. She's so looking forward to your both being at your *rancho* in Brazil."

The aging white face smiled a little. "Hilda," he said in a whisper. "Come here."

I went over to the side of the bed as Uncle Brace moved away. Then I saw von Rucker's hand fumbling and realized he wanted to take my hand. Trying not to show my anger and revulsion, I reached out my hand and took his. *Play along,* my mind told me. So I was going to be as cooperative as I could. My chances of getting away were even less than I had thought. But open defiance would make them nil. "I'm very sorry you're ill," I said.

"It's nothing. That is," he smiled a little, "it's everything—death, I'm afraid."

"Nonsense," Uncle Brace said. He had moved to the other side of the bed and was standing there.

"I'd like to talk to Hilda alone," von Rucker said, turning his head slowly. "Please."

Despite the "please," it was an order. Uncle Brace hesitated a moment. And then, "Of course," he said. "We'll see you later." Then he looked at me once and left. The door had not closed before Williams had come in.

"I want to talk to my daughter alone," von Rucker said. His voice was strained.

"Certainly you may. I shall just sit over here and do some mending. You two just carry on. But I must be here in case you should have any problem. And none of us would want to think that Miss Hilda had caused it." She took some sewing out of a bag she was carrying and put it on a small table by the window. "But first, I'll just check your pulse." After what seemed a long minute she put von Rucker's hand down. "It's much too rapid," she said scoldingly, and looked at me. "He must not be agitated. Please be as calm and cheerful as you can." She said every word as though it carried a meaning beyond the usual, which, of course, it did. Obviously, she was in with Uncle Brace.

"Thank you," von Rucker said, and waited while she plumped up the pillows, made the covers neat, and finally went and sat on the chair beside the little table. The afternoon sun streamed in onto Williams' sewing, and her head was bent over it. But there was no sound in the room and anything that was said could be heard easily.

Von Rucker's hand closed over mine. "Bend down," he whispered.

I bent down.

"Put your ear to my mouth."

Williams got up. "I think that'll be enough now," she said cheerfully. "You must let Baron von Rucker rest. You can come back later in the afternoon."

"I wish to talk to my daughter, and I wish to talk to her alone. You will please go." I could hear the effort it took for him to say that, and I could also hear how short his breath was.

"Now just be calm," she said, and took a syringe out of her pocket. "This'll make you feel better."

"Get out!" he said, and started to rise from the pillows.

He was a dying man—even I could see that—but there was so much power and authority in the way he spoke, for all his short breath and hoarse voice that she backed.

"Go!" he said again. "And if you or Kingsmark comes in until I have finished with speaking to Hilda, then I *will* have another heart attack and that wouldn't fit into your plans at all, would it? Now leave us!"

She quickly left, muttering angrily. At the door she said, "I'll go now, but I'll be back!"

"Now," he said to me, lying back on the pillows, "lean down. I'm not going to get to Brazil and I know it." After a minute he went on. "Try not to hate me. I should not have . . ." he paused, his breathing labored, and then continued, "I should not have tried to see you this way. I don't have much time . . . or strength. Kingsmark is an evil man. I had not seen how evil. They're going to try and make you marry Paul."

"Marry Paul!" I couldn't believe what I was hearing. "But I'm not even old enough to marry."

"In some parts of the world you're more than old enough. They could probably fly in some priest or minister and marry you here or in Sibyl."

"But *why?*"

"Because when I die you will be a very rich young woman. I have left everything I own to you."

I stared at him, not taking it in. Then, "But don't you have a family?"

"No," he whispered. "My wife and I had one child—a son—but he died many years ago. I told you. You're the end of the line."

My mind still hadn't really absorbed it. "Oh, I wish you hadn't. Then they'd let me go. Can't you change your will?" And, of course, the moment I said that, I knew it was impossible. Also that I was being ungrateful. "I'm sorry, Mr. . . . Mr. von Rucker, I didn't mean to sound ungrateful . . . it's just . . ." The blue eyes that had looked so cold when I first met him were on me now, not cold at all. Just sad.

"I was wrong, and I hurt you," I said. "I'm sorry." I saw him fight for his breath. "Don't try to talk," I said, alarmed. I certainly didn't want to cause him to die. Also,

I had a strong feeling that as long as he was alive, Uncle Brace wouldn't do anything to me.

"I suppose," he said, after a minute, "you couldn't bring yourself to call me anything but Mr. von Rucker."

"I know you're a baron."

"I didn't mean that," he spoke more sharply than he had so far. He breathed heavily for a moment. "I think I meant something like 'father.' But then, you already have a father, don't you?"

"Yes." I felt uncomfortable and rather mean, but there *was* only one person in my mind whom I could call "Father." Wordlessly, I nodded.

"And I gather you would not, as I had hoped, be willing to change your name to von Rucker?"

Feeling even meaner I shook my head again. "You see, my father—I mean the man I always thought of as my father—and I've been so close. It would kill him." And yet, and yet, I wondered, anger rising again. This wonderful father was the one who, when he discovered the truth about me, went off to South America and left me to come here.

As though he had read my mind, von Rucker said, "But he left you to come here, didn't he?"

"He didn't know what kind of place it was. It sounded like some super place in the Virgin Islands or Bermuda."

"Did you read the letter?"

"No. Mother told me."

Mother told me. And of course I trusted them. "Don't look like that, Hilda. That letter was carefully composed to give just the impression your family got."

"Well, when Aunt Louisa wrote about the young people and the swimming—"

"Your Aunt Louisa couldn't write her name at this point. You must know that. That letter was written by someone else and she laboriously copied it with her husband standing over her.''

"And all so I could marry Paul.''

"Precisely.'' I could hear his breathing, in, out, for a few minutes. I was still holding his hand, and mine was going to sleep. "Look,'' I said, "my hand's going to sleep. That's why I'm going to take it away. Not because . . .''

"Not because you are tired of holding hands with an old man you don't even know who has brought all this misery on you.'' And I felt his hand slide out of mine.

"No,'' I said, and smiled. "Not because of that.'' I paused and then went on, "How could you do all this planning with a man like Uncle Brace? You said yourself he was evil.''

"I was afraid to write direct, just as I thought if I turned up in New York your father, given his views, which I had taken trouble to find out, would usher me to the door without even listening—and would make sure that you would approach me with hatred. So, instead, I arranged for an American I know, who is at the university in São Paulo and who knows your father, to write to him, telling him the truth about your paternity but conveying it as a widely held belief. Tashoff was fairly sure to come down and see for himself, which would leave you free to come to the island here. . . .'' He paused and rested for a moment.

"So it was you who prompted that letter.''

"Yes. So if you feel deserted by your present family, I am afraid the fault is mine.''

"But how could you use somebody like Uncle Brace?''

"Because he made himself so agreeable, because we had had business contacts—he exports my coffee for me—and because we believe—all of us believe—what we want to believe. After all, you believed what you wanted to believe about that young pilot, didn't you?''

"Yes," I said bitterly. "I did. And I was wrong. When Uncle Brace came to stop him he absolutely buckled."

"I'm sorry." We sat there for a while.

"I wonder why that awful Williams or Uncle Brace hasn't come in. She said she'd be back."

"I imagine because they have found some other way of hearing what we're saying. . . . There could be microphones in the room. It doesn't matter." He looked at me intensely for a moment. Then said, "There's some water in the carafe and a glass over there on the bureau. Could you bring me some?"

I jumped up, poured some water and was coming back with it to the bed when I saw him put his fingers to his lips and then beckon me. I went over "Thank you, my dear," he said, and as I sat down and handed him the glass, pulled me suddenly to him, spilling the water on the bedspread. I opened my mouth but he put his hand over it. Then he took the glass and placed it on the table and pulled me to him again, putting his mouth at my ear.

"Leave now," he whispered, his voice so low I could barely hear it. "There is something more I must do, and I must stay alive long enough to do it. Give me paper and pen from that desk over there and then go. I will send for you. Until then, try not to defy them." Then he leaned back and said in his normal voice, "I seem to have spilled some of the water. I'm sorry. But I'm getting tired. Perhaps I should sleep a little now. I will send for you again, *Liebchen*."

"What does that mean?" I asked in my own normal voice, getting up. I went to the desk and returned with paper and ball-point pen, which I handed to him. He slid them under the covers. That odd, half-smile I noticed before twisted his face. "It means darling."

165

* * *

They were outside, of course. Williams slipped in and Uncle Brace took my arm, but more gently this time. "I must ask you to stay in your room for the time," he said, and I went with him meekly as he marched me upstairs. When we got to my room he opened the door and pushed me in. As I turned, I saw the key in his hand.

"Please," I said. "Can I have Wolf up here? Please?" I hated myself for sounding so submissive, so conciliatory, but I wanted Wolf where I could know he was safe. And then I thought, *conciliatory* . . . just like Steve.

Uncle Brace hesitated. Then, "All right. I'll send him. By the way, have you eaten?"

I shook my head.

"I'll bring a sandwich." And he slammed the door shut.

I went over to the windows which were, of course, open. There was no air conditioning on the island, and if the windows were shut, keeping out the wind that blew constantly, the heat and humidity would have been unbearable. However, though he hadn't closed my windows and locked them, he had placed Raoul just below my room. When I looked down Raoul grinned, showing large, crooked teeth. There was no hope of escape there. I was trying to think of some way around all this when there was a sound at the door, which opened. Wolf leaped in, a hand holding a plate put it on the table by the door and then shut it.

Wolf and I had an affectionate reunion. I managed to eat half the sandwich. Then I sat on my bed and tried to think. It was getting dark outside. I wondered what happened to Pronto, which brought Steve back to my mind, and also brought within me an intense tug-of-war. If I had been deliberately conciliatory to Uncle Brace for a purpose, couldn't that have been true of Steve, too? I wanted to think that, yet

I couldn't help remembering that his uncle's airline seemed to be his chief consideration. And even Uncle Brace said he could have found a way around giving in so easily. *Even Uncle Brace . . .* what on earth was I thinking of? Uncle Brace had his own very large ax to grind, so of course he'd blacken Steve's motives. Von Rucker was right. He was an evil man. Back and forth went the tug-of-war in my head. I wanted so much to believe that Steve didn't cave in just because he lacked guts. On the other hand, I was afraid to . . .

Quite astonishingly I discovered I was drifting off to sleep, and I was also aware for the first time that I'd eaten only half a sandwich since breakfast. Well, I thought, all I had to do was cross the room to get the other half. . . . But it seemed more than I could manage because I was sleepier than I was hungry. In fact . . . At that point, I went to sleep.

When I woke up it was dark outside and felt hours later. I looked at the illuminated hands of my traveling clock: a quarter to ten. Wolf was lying beside me, but had also woken up, because he licked my face. "Yes, thanks a lot. I love you, too," I whispered.

I sat up, listening. People went to bed early at Tradewinds, so I wasn't surprised not to hear anyone moving or people talking. Then I wondered what had happened with von Rucker. Was he still alive? His downstairs bedroom was on the same side as mine, but faced the back.

Getting out of bed I went to the door and listened. Then, slowly, I turned the doorknob and pulled. But the lock held. I was still trapped. Walking soundlessly in my sneakers, I went over to the window. There were no lights on in the room, and because of the bright moonlight, it was much brighter outside than in. Standing so I was hidden by the window curtain, I looked outside to see if Raoul was still there. He was, leaning against a tree, picking his teeth. Well, I thought, that took care of that.

Going over to the table I retrieved the second half of the sandwich and divided it with Wolf. Then I went back to the bed and lay down. I could, of course, turn on the light and read, but a blazing light from my window would tell everyone that I was awake, and I felt, somehow, that if they thought I was asleep they'd be less alert and off their guard.

So I lay there, trying to think of ways to get out. If it weren't for Raoul, I could easily get down from my window. It was only the second floor, and I could use the sheets for a rope as I had read in countless adventures. But Raoul was there, and he was awake. . . . Eventually, he'd have to sleep, but then someone else might be put there. And even if he did fall asleep, and I could let myself down by knotted sheets, how would I get Wolf out? If they found me gone, I was sure they would destroy Wolf out of sheer spite. "I won't leave you, Wolf," I said, gently pulling one of his ears. I knew he understood, because he licked my hand.

As the long, slow minutes passed I thought about Steve, about his dark hair, his bony nose, his green eyes and about how simply wonderful it was when he kissed me. The trouble with thinking about that was that it led to thinking about the moments in the plane when he didn't make a move to help me, or talk to Uncle Brace, or even risk knocking into the car—anything to keep from handing me over. . . . *But Uncle Brace put that idea into your head, so why let him influence you against me?*

It was in Steve's voice that I heard the words. But I couldn't seem to move off that scene in the plane, so I thought about my father instead, and all I could think of was his leaving me to come here to this awful place, just because he thought I was the natural daughter of a German officer. . . . *But his grandmother and two of his uncles whom*

168

*he had known and cared for as a child had died in a concen-
tration camp, put there by the government for which this
man fought.*

Curiously, those words seemed to come in my mother's
voice. She was always pointing out the commonsense view
and putting herself in other people's situations. And then I
thought of my biological father, walking away and leaving
me. . . . This time I could hear my sister Juliet's voice,
as clear as though she were standing at the end of the
bed. . . . *"You know what your problem is—you're just
sorry for yourself."*

"I have good reason," I muttered into my pillow, and
drifted off to sleep again.

I don't know how long I had been asleep when something
woke me. It also woke Wolf, because I felt him sit up beside
me. Then I heard the faint click of the lock and soft
footsteps going away from the door. Wolf was already at the
door and in a second I was with him, turning the knob as
quietly as I could. With the knob turned, I gave a little pull,
and the door opened. To the right down the dark hall I saw
Aunt Louisa walking slowly, one hand against the wall,
steadying herself as she crept back to her room. Quickly,
and as silently as I could, I ran after her and put my arm
around her and my face close to hers. "Thanks, Aunt Louisa," I whispered. "Thanks a lot."

She held me a second. Then she said, her lips next to my
ear, "Go, go quickly now. Somebody'll be back in my
room any time. Now run."

Wolf and I didn't run. But, with my hand under his collar
to keep him from making any noise or running along the
wooden floor where his nails would click against the wood,
we moved inch by inch down the hall, down the stairs and
across to the front door. There I hesitated. Raoul might or
might not be there. He might or might not be asleep. At that

point I remembered the French doors leading out of one of the wings, and we turned and started down the long west hall. If it had not been for Raoul, it would have been far less nerve-racking to go out the front door, because the west hall was lined with doors behind which might be servants or guards. But, as we crept by on the carpet that was down the center, I reminded myself that Raoul's presence outside the front was almost a certainty, whereas the rooms we were passing could be empty. It was a comforting thought, and I concentrated on it to keep up my spirits.

Eventually we were past and reached the tall, glass paneled doors. I stared at the knob in the dim light from the moon outside. It could, of course, be locked, and then Wolf and I would have to start all over again. But, after I'd been looking at it for a while, I saw that it was simply bolted. Gently, quietly, I eased back the bolt and turned the knob. The door opened. Still holding Wolf, I tiptoed out, and closed the door after me.

"Now Wolf," I whispered, "let's get out of here."

To run across the moonlit drive, or tennis court or pool area would be madness. The only chance Wolf and I had was to hug the trees to our left until we got to the path slightly below the house that transversed the woods and led to the main island road. Walking as quickly as I dared, or could, still leading Wolf, I moved west and then north along the shadowed edge of the mini-forest that covered so much of the island.

Where I was going to go, I wasn't sure. I certainly could not leave the island without the aid of either a plane or a boat. Most of the residents would be terrified to give me any refuge because of what Uncle Brace could, and undoubtedly would, do to them. And then I thought of José. Uncle Brace would be as merciless to him as he would to anyone else, but I remembered that José was not as helpless. He was a teacher, and a good one, according to Steve, and if he lost his job on Maenad, then he could have one at the university on Sibyl. So Wolf and I would make for José's barn. Which meant, of course, that we had to get down to the village, a distance of some seven miles. Well, I thought, here was where all the jogging Father and I did in Central Park would come in useful. I was in better shape than most. But I would not dare to run until we reached the main road. The turf and the path were too dark, too uneven and too dangerous underfoot to do anything but walk as rapidly as possible.

The thought of my father had sent a pang through me. Inevitably, I thought of Steve and finally the man lying in the bed up at the big house. All three, I thought angrily, had let me down in the crunch. Well, I would make it somehow on my own. It was nice to believe that I could, and the decision made me feel better in one way, but worse in another. I decided that if you're used to trusting people, learning not to trust them was unpleasant and depressing.

How long it took to skirt the cleared area around the house and to reach the path leading through the woods to the main drive I didn't know. It could have been ten minutes or fifty. But I kept up as rapid a pace as I could, overwhelmingly aware that at any moment someone could try the door to my bedroom at Tradewinds and make the discovery that I had gone. After that, search parties would be sent out, and I didn't know how long Wolf and I could keep hidden. The path through the woods was not an experience that I enjoyed at all. Luckily, the ground itself was fairly even, though almost completely dark. A slight glimmer of light filtered through the trees here and there, just enough to keep me from being in black darkness. So I walked slowly and carefully. Once a twig snapped, and I froze. I could feel Wolf next to my legs, and heard the beginning of a growl start deep in his chest.

"Quiet!" I whispered, and put my hand around his muzzle.

Another time something started up in the woods at my left, and I felt as though I jumped about six feet.

Eventually, we reached the drive, and in the brilliant moonlight splashing down the asphalt, it felt almost as though it were noon.

"Okay Wolf, now we run!" And I let go of his collar.

Not only was I in good condition, but the road went gently downhill. Wolf and I made excellent time. I kept talking to him quietly to keep him as near me as possible. I had no leash, and had forgotten to bring anything that could serve as a substitute. But I did not want him to go off exploring through the woods into the center of the island. There were many out there who could not discriminate between Wolf and the murderous dogs trained by Schmidt so I kept on my running commentary which seemed to keep him beside me listening.

I had run in several mini-marathons in New York, and now made good time, my legs eating up the miles, Wolf trotting effortlessly beside me. And I was beginning to get into that semihypnotized state that runners sometimes experience when a sound snapped me back to reality: a car was coming towards us.

"Wolf, quick, into the trees!"

Dragging him by his collar, I ducked into the trees that lined the highway, crouching down and keeping my hand in Wolf's collar. If Uncle Brace or Williams had found my door open, with me gone, there was nothing to prevent them from calling someone at the other end of the island, and arranging to have two search parties close in on us.

"Quiet, quiet now!" I whispered, as the car drew nearer and nearer, coming at a fairly high speed.

As they got nearer I saw it was not one car but three, all of them Jeeps. The first Jeep was speeding past before I took in the fact that Steve was driving the Jeep and sitting beside him was my father.

12

I leaped up and tore to the road, shouting, "Daddy! Father! It's me, Hilda! Stop!"

In the still night my voice rang out loud and clear. The third Jeep had passed before they all slowed and stopped.

"Daddy!" I cried out again. "It's me, Hilda!" And I started running with Wolf beside me. As I ran past I saw the two rear Jeeps filled with men in uniform. By the time I came near the front Jeep, they all got out of the Jeeps. A thin wiry figure detached itself from the bunched group and started running towards me.

"Hilda!" my father yelled. We met halfway. And then we were hugging and my father was telling me how sorry he was that he had been such a pig-headed, prejudiced idiot. "Instead of thinking about you and how you would feel, I acted on a prejudice about the idea of your having a German father. I'm sorry, darling, really sorry."

"You ran away and left me!" I said, crying now out of relief and happiness.

"Yes, I did. Your mother, who wasn't happy about any of it, even when we thought they were all right, kept telling me every hour on the hour that we should be here with you.

And that was before we heard about the horror show you were encountering here.''

''How did you find out?''

''Your friend Steve Barrington got on the phone and called the apartment, the publishing house, the New York police, the State Department and a few other places, and found out we were in Miami, waiting for a plane to New York and told us the kind of mess you'd walked into. The only thing I can say in our defense is that we were on our way here anyway. I feel terrible. I truly didn't know. I went down to confront this Nazi who seems to be your biological father—''

''He isn't a Nazi, Daddy,'' I said wiping my nose on my sleeve because, as usual, I didn't have a handkerchief.

''Here, take this. That's a revolting thing to do. No, I gather he isn't. In any case, it's no excuse for the way I treated you. Please forgive me.'' He hugged me so hard my ribs hurt, but I didn't care. There was something I had to know. ''Father, do you love me as much as you would if I were your real, biological daughter?''

''Of course I do! Love doesn't have a thing to do with biology.

''Oh, God! I wish I'd had the brains to listen to your mother. She wanted to tell you from the beginning. But I was working on one of my wonderful theories about environment and heredity, and talked her out of it. You know about me and my theories, don't you? And the fact that we were living abroad at the time made it easy. We simply came back with our three-year-old daughter. Who was to know? I'm sorry, baby.''

I gave him another hug, feeling incomparably better. He was sounding just like his old self, and I could easily imagine the kind of theoretical argument he put forward for not doing something that Mother's common sense told her they ought to do. "Yes," I said. "You may have the brains, but Mother has the wisdom."

I could see my father wince. "True, very true, and sobering." He looked down. "And who is this?"

"This" was Wolf, who, tired of being left out of the affection going around, had put his paws up on my chest and was trying to lick my face.

"This is Wolf. He's mine." I looked at Father and said defiantly, "I'm taking him home."

"Your mother—"

"Mother can have injections the way she did when we kept her sister's dog for three months. Remember?"

"I thought all the Kingsmark dogs were savage," one of the uniformed men said.

"This one is an exception," Steve said, strolling up.

"Hi!" I said. "And a million thanks." I went over and hugged and kissed him. "I'm always doing this to you," I said. "But I have something to confess."

"You thought I welshed out on you, didn't you?"

I nodded. He gave me a quick hug and kiss and then we separated. I could see him eyeing my father.

"Daddy," I said. "Without Steve I'd still be in that awful place."

"You see," Steve said, "I knew there were a couple of things I could try that might help you out immediately. But there was a good chance they wouldn't work. And if they didn't, I might not be able to get back to Sibyl where I *knew* I could get help. But I wanted that maniac to think I was more concerned about my uncle's airline and my own skin. He understands that, and it wouldn't be hard to make him believe it."

"He told me you should have rammed his car."

"So two gasoline tanks could have exploded? And you swallowed that?"

"I never even thought of that. I'm truly sorry," I said. "Von Rucker said they wanted me to marry Paul, which is why Uncle Brace was running you down."

"Good God, why?" Father asked.

"Because von Rucker said he was leaving me everything and I'd be rich."

My father and Steve stared at me. Then Father said, "Well, it makes sense out of why the Kingsmarks were so involved."

"We had better be going," one of the uniformed men said in his soft island voice.

"Who are these?" I asked.

"Sibyl police. They flew over in their own plane, and got the Jeeps out of the garage here where they keep them locked up. How's your Aunt Louisa? And how's von Rucker?"

"Von Rucker had a second heart attack and is dying, I'm certain. He's very sorry he used Uncle Brace and apologized to me. He wanted me to call him Father, just once. I felt mean, but I couldn't do it."

My father ruffled my hair. "I'd be lying if I didn't say I was glad." He looked at me for a moment. "Did you feel any . . . any kinship with him, at all?"

"No. I remembered something . . . and it was like that nightmare I sometimes have. I guess I did remember it, somewhere." And I told him about my memory of his walking away. "But I was so desperate to get off the island and get home and I didn't have time to feel anything but that. Did you go down to South America to find out about him— and me?"

"Yes. I made up the story about a book on guerrillas— there wasn't one. But I had to have an excuse for going there. I'll tell you all about it later—when we get home. I don't think this is the time or place, and the police there want to arrest your dear Uncle Brace.''

"Hurray!" I said. And then, "Why?"

"Among other things, for drug smuggling. They had a search warrant and went through his warehouses there on the airfield. There they found all kinds of goodies—cocaine, and heroin, to mention a few."

"I wonder . . . I'm sure Mr. von Rucker didn't know that," I said, surprised at how much I wanted that to be true.

My father looked at me. "It would bother you if he did know?"

"Yes."

The police from the other Jeeps came up. "We're going to the house," one of them said to Father. "We would rather you and your daughter returned to Sibyl. Steve here can fly you."

"All right," my father said. "Although I'd take great pleasure in telling Kingsmark what I thought of him. And I'd like . . . I'd like to meet von Rucker."

"No," I said. "I want us to go with the police."

"But why?" the policeman asked. "We don't have to tell you how dangerous this man is. We've been trying to get something on him for a long time, but when Steve said you were being held against your will, it was the first time we had anything we could act on. It would be foolish for you to expose yourself like that."

But something was pushing me hard. Now that I was free, and had my real father and Steve with me, I found I couldn't just go off as though von Rucker didn't matter.

"I have to go," I said stubbornly. "Daddy, please understand."

"I'll try," he said. Then, after a minute, "I guess that means we go with you."

Steve and I sat in front and Father in the back. Wolf sat on my lap blocking out my view. Once, Steve glanced at me and smiled. Then he reached out and took my hand, and held it for a moment.

The house was lit up when we drove to the bottom of the front steps. The police went ahead of us. Then Father, Steve, Wolf and I followed. As the police fanned out through the house, I led the way to von Rucker's bedroom.

Just as I reached the door to open it, I knew suddenly that he was dead. "He's dead," I said to Father.

"How do you know?"

"I don't know. But I know."

I opened the door. Von Rucker was lying there, very much the same as when I had last seen him. Yet I knew that he was no longer part of the body lying against the pillows, the eyes closed. And then, as I looked, something strange happened to me. At no point before had I felt any sense of kinship with him, even though I could see I resembled him in face and coloring and build. Yet now, when he was dead, something tugged at me, and I found myself crying.

Father put his arm around me. "You know, Hilda, didn't expect him to look so much like you, or I guess should put it the other way around."

"Mr. Tashoff," the chief policeman said, coming into the room. "Would you please come at once into the study There's . . . well, please come in. All of you."

"What's up?" Father said.

"Just follow me, please."

"I'll be there in a minute," I said.

"All right." The officer hesitated, then left with Father Steve was there with me. "Do you want me to go?"

"No." I went over to the bed. "Steve, it's so weird. A the time I was here I felt nothing but . . . but dislike, eve revulsion. I guess I was scared. Now . . . I wish I could ta to him a minute. Tell him I don't hate him. He was so sad.

"He probably knows how you feel. I think we'd better be going after the others."

"Yes. All right." I leaned over and kissed von Rucker on the cheek. "Good-bye . . . Father," I said finally, and wondered if Steve was right: if somewhere he knew I called him that.

Then Steve and I went after the others through the study and dining room, down the long hall to Brace Kingsmark's study, following the lights and the sounds of voices. When we got there we stopped in the doorway. I stared, feeling a little sick. Brace Kingsmark was lying on the floor, blood coming out of a cut on his head and from his mouth. Then I saw the front of his chest was covered with blood. He, too, was dead. Sitting in her armchair, a revolver in her hand, was Aunt Louisa, looking less drugged than I had ever seen her.

The chief police officer looked up briefly as we came in. Then he turned back to Aunt Louisa. "Now tell us what happened."

Aunt Louisa said, "He was going after Hilda to bring her back. I had to stop him. I pretended to be asleep the last time they came to give me an injection. It worked. I suppose they were distracted. So I was able to get hold of Brace's pistol. I came down here. Brace was on the telephone, trying to have Hilda stopped. I started to go over to him. He saw me and came after me. He said I was to go upstairs and he and Williams would come and give me another injection. I told him he was never going to give me another injection. He just laughed and lunged towards me. So I shot him."

I went over and put my arm around her.

"How are you, child?"

"I'm . . . I'm fine." I still couldn't believe what I saw. "Did you really shoot Uncle Brace?"

"I did. My one regret is that I didn't do it much sooner.

But he always kept me doped up. Now, thanks to him I'm a drug addict, and I'm going to have to get off of it."

"We'll take you back to the States," I said.

"I'm afraid not," the officer said. "We must put her in custody in Sibyl."

"Surely she'll be exonerated on account of her condition," my father said. "How is it they phrase it in the English courts? 'Being of unsound mind'?"

"My mind isn't unsound," Aunt Louisa said. "This is the best thing I ever did for myself or anyone else."

"You can see the American consul and talk to the authorities in Sibyl," the officer said.

"I'm sure my wife—who is Mrs. Kingsmark's cousin—would like to see that she goes to a hospital in the States."

"We have hospitals here," the officer smiled. "However, as I said, this is a matter for you and the consul and the authorities to work out." He paused, "I can't imagine anyone in the islands not believing it was self-defense."

At that point two men in white jackets came in with a stretcher. They put it down, looked towards the police officer, who nodded. Bending, they picked up Uncle Brace by the shoulders and ankles and placed him on the stretcher, covered him with a sheet and carried him out.

For a moment, before they pulled up the sheet, I saw his face. The eyes were still open and staring. I'd never seen a dead person before, and now, in the last hour, I'd seen two. It made me feel strangely vulnerable. Death was no longer something I read about in the paper or heard about on television. I'd seen it. I was glad Uncle Brace was dead. I couldn't imagine that he'd ever done anything good. I was sad that von Rucker had died, although I felt that his death was not shameful, as Uncle Brace's was. And I still didn't know how I felt about being his natural daughter.

"Where is Williams?" I asked. "And Paul?"

"They appear to have run away," the chief policeman said. "And one of the cars is missing."

"But wouldn't you have run into them? There's only one road."

"They could have taken the road going up to the peak, and then come down on the east side of the island, with the idea of avoiding us. But our men are in charge at the airfield, so they won't get far."

I suddenly found myself feeling sorry for Paul. "I don't think Paul actually did anything."

"Nothing, except confiscate for Brace the letter you received from your parents," Aunt Louisa said.

"So there was a letter!"

"Oh yes."

"But why didn't Uncle Brace want me to get it?"

"They—your parents—might have wanted you to come home. He couldn't take the risk."

"What happened to the letter?"

"It was destroyed. Anyway, Paul's just a tiresome young man who takes on the color of anyone around who's in authority. But he's had a wretched life, so he isn't completely to blame. If I don't die or go to jail or have a nervous breakdown or get locked up for my own good and the public good, I'll see what I can do for him."

My father looked at her. "Hilda said von Rucker told her that he'd left everything to her. Is that true?"

"Yes, poor child."

"Why 'poor'?" the policeman said. "Many would be glad." He glanced at me. "You will own, among other things, a coffee plantation."

"What am I going to do with that?" I asked.

"Sell it?" Steve said. He was standing by the door.

"Or she could use it as the base of a local liberation front," my father said, only half kidding.

181

"Well," the policeman went on, "we found an addition to the will on Baron von Rucker's night table." He took a piece of paper out of his pocket. "He says he had originally named Brace Kingsmark as the trustee until Miss Hilda comes of age, but he now prefers you to be."

"Well now," Father said. "We're going to have to fend off people who want to marry you for your money." I knew he was only making a poor joke because he was upset. He had always looked upon vast properties as subversive.

But I said anyway, "I hope you're not saying that that's the only reason anybody'd want to marry me."

"I can promise you it isn't," Steve said.

Father glanced at him. "Hummmm." Then he looked at me. "I guess we'd better go."

"Come on, Wolf," I said. Wolf, who had been sitting near me, watching us, got up and came over.

Father looked at him with less than enthusiasm. "Do we have to take him? I'm not crazy about animals in a New York apartment, you know."

"So it wasn't just Mother's allergy."

He looked a little abashed. "Not entirely. Come on, Hilda. He's used to being outdoors. Let's leave him here."

"He'll be killed. Besides . . ." I knew I was a little angry, but I was not prepared for what popped out of my mouth next. "My other father gave him to me."

Father's head snapped up. He stared at me in astonishment and some kind of hurt. My anger broke. "Oh Daddy, I'm so confused. I don't know what I feel."

He came over and put his hands on my shoulders. "We'll work it out. After all, it's my fault you didn't know about . . . about your background." He looked down. "All right, hound. *Andiamo!*"

Then he raised his head and he and I looked at one another for another moment. I knew then that I had accepted my relationship to von Rucker. And I had also accepted that it did, in some way, alter my relationship to the man I had always called Father. A feeling of sadness and loss swept over me. For a moment it was as though I were living again my old nightmare: the tall figure stalking out of my life, and me, desolate and crying, running after him. Only now it was memory, not a dream, and I didn't know whether the loss I now felt was the old one, or because the man I had always known as my father I now knew was not.

But the quick understanding that had always been between us was still there. My father put his hand on my shoulder and gently shook it. "It's all right, Hilda. Really." He grinned. "We'll survive."

As we were all leaving I said, "Steve's coming to the States to college."

Father glanced over to him. "Good for you. Where are you going?"

Steve grinned. "I was leaning towards Harvard. But in the last few days I've come to see Columbia as more my choice."

Father's eyes flickered over to me. "I wonder why," he said drily. "I can see now that if it's not one upheaval in our life it'll probably be another."

He grinned and ruffled my hair. "It goes with having a daughter who's seventeen. C'mon!"

"Yes, Daddy," I said. "Let's go."

ABOUT THE AUTHOR

Isabelle Holland, the daughter of an American diplomatic officer, was born in Switzerland. Miss Holland was educated in England and the United States and spent a number of years in publishing before turning to writing as a career. Her most recent adult novel is FLIGHT OF THE ARCHANGEL. Her most recent young adult novel is JENNY KISS'D ME.

Young people learning to cope with the feelings and contradictions of growing up...

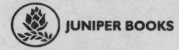 **JUNIPER BOOKS**